Is That a Glow-in-the-Dark BUNNY In Your Pillowcase?

**Check out these other
outrageous adventures
by Todd Strasser!**

Is That a Dead Dog
in Your Locker?

Is That a Sick Cat
in Your Backpack?

Is That a Glow-in-the-Dark Bunny in Your Pillowcase?

TODD STRASSER

SCHOLASTIC INC.
New York Toronto London Auckland Sydney
Mexico City New Delhi Hong Kong Buenos Aires

This book is dedicated to the
memory of Kurt Vonnegut, Jr.,
who demonstrated just how funny
and poignant writing can be.

No part of this publication may be reproduced, stored in a retrieval system, or transmitted in any form or by any means, electronic, mechanical, photocopying, recording, or otherwise, without written permission of the publisher. For information regarding permission, write to Scholastic Inc., Attention: Permissions Department, 557 Broadway, New York, NY 10012.

ISBN-13: 978-0-439-77696-7
ISBN-10: 0-439-77696-1

Text copyright © 2007 by Todd Strasser.

All rights reserved. Published by Scholastic Inc. SCHOLASTIC, APPLE PAPERBACKS, and associated logos are trademarks and/or registered trademarks of Scholastic Inc.

12 11 10 9 8 7 6 5 4 3   9 10 11 12 13 14/0

Printed in the U.S.A.   40
This edition first printing, August 2009

ACKNOWLEDGMENTS

The author would like to acknowledge the following people who stuck with him during the many years of terrible struggle and agonizing effort that went into creating this priceless work of literature: Alex Silver for his extensive knowledge of glow-in-the-dark bunnies. Abby Silver for her extensive knowledge of candy. Gina Shaw, Suzanne Nelson, and Matt Ringler for their patient tolerance. Mr. Gene Splicing for his contributions to science. Ms. Kath A. Rabbett for the invention of the Rab-o-Vac and Rab-o-Rake. However, the author now regrets that he acknowledged Catherine Zeta-Jones in his last book.

AUTHOR'S RHYMING GUARANTEE IN HAIKU FORM

RHYMING GUARANTEE:
This book is UNDERPANTS and
UNDERWEAR free. See?

AUTHOR'S NOTE

Welcome to the third book in the Tardy Boys series. With great regret, the author must admit that, he can no longer claim to have written THE SHORTEST SERIES EVER.

However, there is a growing body of evidence that this is quickly becoming THE FASTEST SERIES EVER.

Kids are reading the Tardy Boys books in record time. Many have finished a Tardy Boys book in less than one hour!

Currently, the record holder for *Is That a Dead Dog in Your Locker?* is Turner D. Paige, of Lickety Split, Utah, with a time of 48 minutes and 27 seconds.

The record holder for *Is That a Sick Cat in Your Backpack?* is Skip Toothy End of Hurryup, Maine, with a time of 49 minutes and 42 seconds.

Would you like to be the FASTEST FINISHER of *Is That a Glow-in-the-Dark Bunny in Your Pillowcase?* If so, act now. Be one of the first on your block. If you can't be first, try to be second. If you can't be second, move to another block. But whatever you do, don't grow a body of evidence.

Send your fastest time to:

Ms. Lo Compry-Hensen
P.O. Box 789
Haste-Makes-Waste, NY

INTRODUCTION

Winter was over, and the Alien Cats from Planet Hiss in the Feline Galaxy were no longer a threat to Earth. Spring and summer had also passed, and a new school year had begun. Wade and Leyton Tardy were still attending The School With No Name and still had Ms. Fitt for a teacher.

The Tardy Boys' parents were still being held captive by aliens somewhere in the universe, and back on Earth Catherine Zeta-Jones didn't show up for her meeting with the author, so he was thinking of

dedicating a book to Scarlett Johansson instead. Fibby Mandible was still taking Herbal Sodium Pentothal for her fur allergy, and her mother, Ulna, was still screaming and threatening to sue everyone in sight.

Assistant Principal Snout was still wearing blue latex gloves so that he would not have to touch germ-ridden students and bright yellow earplugs to protect his delicate ears from THE SHRIEK OF ULNA MANDIBLE.

Olga Shotput, the school's silver-medal-winning janitor, still wished she could win the gold medal in custodianship, and still waters still ran deep.

And yet, some things were different.

THE
KING
OF
CANDY

It was a few days before Halloween. Around the Tardy Boys' neighborhood, the leaves on the trees were turning yellow and red. Some people wore sweaters or light jackets. Wade, Leyton, and TJ Tardy wore hoodies as they walked along the sidewalk mapping out the best route for trick-or-treating on Halloween night.

"Why do we have to make a map?" asked young TJ Tardy. "Why can't we just go trick-or-treating like everyone else?"

"Because this year we have a small window of opportunity," said Wade, who was thin and scrawny with dark unruly hair, but whose skull was packed with brain cells. "We have to collect as much candy as possible in a short period of time."

"Can't we get a larger window?" asked TJ.

"No," said Wade. "The town has passed a new law that kids can only trick-or-treat from five in the afternoon until eight at night. It really stinks."

"What's that got to do with windows?" asked Leyton, who was handsome, blond, and muscular, but whose skull was SUPPOSEDLY so empty that monkeys could swing from tree branch to tree branch.

"I'll explain later," said Wade. He stopped outside a big yellow house with black shutters. On the front porch were three Jack-o'-lanterns and a plastic glow-in-the-dark skeleton. Cutouts of black cats and witches on brooms were taped to the windows, and the shrubs in the front yard were covered with purple spider-webbing.

"They'll have a lot of candy," Wade said, circling the house on his map.

"Because they have big windows?" Leyton guessed.

"No," said Wade.

"Then how can you tell they'll have a lot of candy?" asked TJ.

"They wouldn't put out all those

Halloween decorations and then skimp on candy," Wade said.

Next to the big yellow house was a small red house with green shutters and no decorations. "What about that house?" asked TJ.

"No way," said Wade.

"Because the windows are too small?" said Leyton.

"Forget the windows!" Wade snapped.

Leyton crossed his arms and glowered. He hated when his brother snapped at him.

"And forget that house, too, right?" TJ said, pointing at a green house with red shutters, medium-size windows, and no decorations.

"That one could be a possibility," said Wade.

"But it's got no decorations," said TJ.

"See the FOR SALE sign?" Wade said. "If they're trying to sell that house, they want it to look nice. They may wait until the last minute to put up their Halloween decorations. We'll have to check that one again in a couple of days."

"Wow," said TJ. "I never knew trick-or-treating could be so complicated."

"It's just like science," Wade said. "There's a hypothesis and —"

"A hypo-who?" interrupted TJ.

"A hypothesis," said Wade. "You say it like this: *hi-pah-the-sis*. It's like a theory. My hypothesis is that the more Halloween decorations a house has, the more candy they give out. And the person who collects the most candy will win the King of Candy Contest."

Just then the streetlights went on. It was starting to get dark.

"Shouldn't we go home?" TJ asked.

"Yes, but let's stop by Daisy's on the way," Wade said. "She has something she wants to show me."

The Tardy Boys headed toward their friend Daisy Peduncle's house. Daisy lived in a big, old white house with a porch and big windows. They were crossing Daisy's lawn when TJ suddenly stopped.

"Look!" he gasped.

THE GLOW-IN-THE-DARK BUNNY MYSTERY

TJ pointed at a large, dark green bush. "That's where it was!"

"Where what was?" Wade asked.

"Go look," said TJ.

Wade and Leyton went behind the bush and looked.

"Do you see it?" asked TJ.

"I see a bush," said Wade.

"And some grass," added Leyton.

"Are you sure?" TJ asked.

"Yeah, we're sure," said Wade as he and Leyton walked back toward their little brother. "What did you see?"

"I can't tell you," said TJ.

"Why not?" asked Wade.

"You'll never believe me," said the youngest Tardy Boy.

"Yes, we will," said Leyton.

"No, you won't," said TJ.

"Come on, TJ, what did you see?" said Wade.

TJ shook his head.

"We promise we'll believe you," said Leyton.

"You mean it?" asked TJ.

"Yes, just tell us already," Wade said impatiently.

"Are you *sure* you promise?" asked TJ.

"For Pete's sake, tell us," Wade grunted irritably.

"Who's Pete?" asked Leyton.

"Be quiet!" Wade snapped.

"You don't have to be such a jerk," Leyton complained. "All I did was ask who Pete was."

"Pete has nothing to do with this," Wade said.

"So he's like a window, too?" guessed Leyton.

Wade glared as if Leyton was so dim-witted he'd probably put his watch in the bank to save time, so numskulled he'd need half an hour to make minute rice, and so brainless he'd sit on the TV and watch the couch.

That made Leyton mad. He made a fist and shook it at his brother. "You think you're so smart just because you're the one who was *born* with all the brains. But you don't know everything. Someday you're going to be really surprised. And why are you in such a bad mood anyway?"

"I'm in a bad mood because we have no costumes for Halloween," Wade replied.

"Well, you don't have to get mad at me about that," Leyton said.

Wade knew that was true. He turned back to TJ. "For the last time, what did you see?"

TJ took a deep breath and let it out slowly. "I saw . . . a bunny."

"So?" said Wade. "Why wouldn't we believe that?"

"Because it wasn't a regular bunny," said TJ.

"What kind was it?" asked Leyton.

TJ pressed his lips tightly together.

"Look, I'm tired of this game," Wade grumbled. "Either you tell us right now or don't tell us at all."

"Okay, okay," said TJ. "It was . . . a light green glow-in-the-dark bunny."

Wade and Leyton stared at their little brother.

"You want us to believe you saw a light green glow-in-the-dark bunny?" Wade said with a smirk.

"You *promised!*" TJ cried.

Wade rolled his eyes in disbelief.

"But I saw it!" TJ insisted. He looked at Leyton. "You believe me, don't you?"

Leyton wanted to believe his little brother because he was angry at Wade and wanted Wade to be wrong about everything. But even Leyton had his doubts. "Sorry, little dude," he said, "but light green glow-in-the-dark bunnies only exist in cartoons."

"Then maybe we're in a cartoon!" TJ said.

Leyton shook his head patiently. "If we were in a cartoon, we'd be interrupted by commercials."

"Not if we were on cable," said TJ.

Leyton placed his hand gently on his little brother's shoulder. "Now listen carefully, TJ. We don't pay for cable. And that means this isn't a cartoon, and you didn't see a light green glow-in-the-dark bunny."

TJ's shoulders sagged and he hung his head. "I guess you're right. Thanks for explaining it to me, Leyton."

FLASHBACK

(*We now travel back in time.*)

One day the previous winter — just after Leyton and Skinny Kitty saved the world from the attack of the Alien Cats from Planet Hiss — Leyton and Daisy sat in the school library studying for a big test on the scientific method.

While Daisy studied, Leyton scratched

his head and bit his lip. His eyes darted toward the windows and bookshelves and other tables — everywhere except the book he was supposed to be studying.

Finally, Daisy asked, "What's wrong, Leyton?"

"I can't study," Leyton said.

"Why not?" asked Daisy.

Leyton wasn't sure if he should tell her. The reason he couldn't study had always been his deepest, darkest secret. But he knew that if he never told anyone, then he would never get any help and would have this problem his whole life. And if there was one person he could trust not to laugh at him, it was Daisy.

"If I tell you, will you promise not to make fun of me or tell anyone else?" Leyton asked.

Daisy lifted her rose-colored granny glasses. She reached across the table and placed her hand on his to reassure him. "Leyton, if you want me to keep a secret, then I promise I will never, ever tell anyone."

"Thanks," said Leyton. "The reason I can't study is . . . my skull is empty."

Daisy frowned. "Leyton, that can't be true."

"It is," Leyton said. "Other people have brains in their skulls, but in my skull are vast empty spaces and trees where monkeys swing from branches."

"Who told you that?" Daisy asked.

"Wade," Leyton answered. "He said that when we were born I got big muscles, good looks, and blond hair. But he got the brains. He said that's what happens with fraternal twins. Maybe I should just be happy that I got big muscles and blond hair and good looks, but I really wish there was a way I could get some brains because it's no fun having an empty skull with monkeys swinging around."

Daisy sighed sadly. "Leyton, what if you're smarter than you think?"

Leyton shook his head. "If I had brains, I'd know it."

It was obvious that Leyton was convinced that he had no brains. Daisy wished she could prove to him that he was wrong, but the only way to do that would be to drill a tiny orifice in his skull and show him the brains inside. But doing that in the library would be very messy, and Assistant Principal Snout really hated it when students drilled tiny holes in one another's heads.

Besides, she'd left her drill at home
that day.

Then Daisy had a truly brilliant idea.
"Wait, Leyton, just because you weren't
born with brains doesn't mean you can't
get some now."

Leyton straightened up in surprise.
"How?"

"Well, uh . . ." Daisy had to think of an
answer fast. "You could grow them."

"You mean like in a jar or something?"
Leyton asked.

"No, you'd grow them in your head,"
said Daisy.

Leyton frowned. "I can do that?"

"Sure," said Daisy. "All you need is
Brain Food."

"What's Brain Food?" Leyton asked.

"Fish," said Daisy.

And so, ever since the previous winter,

Leyton had been eating Brain Food. All through the spring and summer he'd been eating it. And now, instead of vast empty spaces, trees, and monkeys, inside Leyton's skull were billions of brand-new, teensy-weensy, itsy-bitsy, baby brain cells. It was only a matter of time until they would begin jiggling and vibrating and having billions of brand-new, teensy-weensy, itsy-bitsy, baby ideas.

PRITTY

(We now return to the present — a few days before Halloween. Isn't time travel fun?)

The lights by Daisy's front door went on, and Daisy came out on the porch barefoot and wearing a bright yellow tie-dyed sundress. Her long brown hair was braided, and she wore her rose-colored granny glasses. "Is someone out there?" she called into the dark.

"Wade, Leyton, and TJ," said Wade as he and his brothers came out of the shadows and climbed the steps up the porch. On the porch were pumpkins with faces painted on them. A scarecrow stuffed with straw sat in a rocking chair.

"Why were you out on the lawn?" Daisy asked.

"We were mapping our Halloween route so that we can get the maximum amount of candy," said Wade.

"Hey," said TJ. "Shouldn't we add Daisy's house to the list? After all, there are lots of Halloween decorations here."

"Uh, I don't think so," said Wade.

TJ looked at Daisy. "Won't your house have candy on Halloween?"

"We'll be giving out homegrown organic carrots," Daisy said.

"That's not candy," said TJ.

"We don't believe in candy," said Daisy.

"So, uh, Daisy," Wade said. "At school today, you said there was something you wanted to show me."

"Oh, right," Daisy said. "Wait here. I'll be right back."

As soon as Daisy left the porch, TJ turned to his older brothers and asked in a low voice, "How can anyone not believe in candy?"

"Her parents are hippies," Wade answered in a whisper.

"What's a hippie?" asked TJ.

"Someone who believes in flower power," said Wade.

"What's flower power?" asked TJ.

Before Wade could answer, Daisy came back to the front door with a folded piece of notebook paper. "I found this in my locker today."

Wade unfolded the paper. On it was a poem:

To Daisy from a Secret Admirer

Every day at school when you walk by
I feel an ache in my heart and the need to sigh.
It kills me that I cannot talk to you.
I wish every day I could walk with you.
You are the sweetest girl in the whole school.
Anyone who doesn't know that is a fool.
Even if we lived in the biggest, most crowded city
There would never be another girl as pritty.

A
BOY
ON
A
MISSION

"What's a secret admirer?" asked TJ.

"It's someone who likes Daisy but is afraid to say so," said Wade.

"Why would he be afraid?" asked TJ.

"Because he's worried that Daisy might not like him back," said Wade.

"I wonder who it is," said Leyton.

"Someone who doesn't know how to spell the word *pretty*," said TJ.

"Do you have any idea who it is?" Wade asked Daisy.

"No," said Daisy. "I was hoping you'd know."

The Tardy Boys shook their heads. They didn't know any secret admirers.

"Maybe we'll find out on Halloween night," Leyton said. "Because the secret admirer might wear a Secret Admirer costume."

Wade and the others frowned. "What does a Secret Admirer costume look like?" asked Daisy.

Leyton scratched his head and waited to see if it was time for all the brand-new, teensy-weensy, itsy-bitsy, baby brain cells to start jiggling and vibrating and coming up with ideas. But the time had not yet come.

"What's your Halloween costume going to be?" TJ asked Daisy.

"I'm going to be a windmill," said Daisy. "Because it's important for people to know about alternative energy sources. What are you going to be?"

"I'm going to be an Atomic Wedgie because it's important for people to know about alternative uses for undergarments," said TJ.

"And what about you two?" Daisy asked Wade and Leyton.

"We don't have much money for costumes," said Wade.

"You don't need money," said Daisy. "You can make costumes out of old things you find lying around the house."

"The only things lying around our house are broken bicycles, smashed skateboards, bent Razor scooters, partly burned sofas, and broken toilets," said Wade.

"Then you can make costumes out of things lying around other people's houses," Daisy suggested.

Daisy's mother came to the door. Her long gray hair was braided, and she wore lots of silver and turquoise jewelry. "Peace and love, boys," she said, making the peace sign with her fingers.

"Peace and love, Mrs. Peduncle," said the Tardy Boys.

"Would you please excuse Daisy," her mother said. "It's time for our evening meditation."

The Tardy Boys told Daisy they would see her tomorrow and left.

"I guess we'll have to make our Halloween costumes out of things from other people's houses," Wade said as they walked through the dark toward home.

"Then this could be our lucky night," said TJ. "Because tomorrow is garbage pickup day, and tonight a lot of people are putting out the stuff they don't want."

As the Tardy Boys walked home, they looked at the things other people were throwing out. They found broken computers, busted lamps, bags of raked leaves, cracked mirrors, and one Extra-Large Mens Jockey-Style Undergarment still in its original packaging.

"Whoa, this sure is *your* lucky night," Leyton told TJ.

"See?" TJ said excitedly as he tucked the Extra-Large Mens Jockey-Style Undergarment under his arm. "Daisy was right. We'll find everything we need right here on the street."

The Tardy Boys kept looking through the piles of garbage. Soon, they were only a few houses away from home.

"I hate to say it, TJ," said Wade, "but it doesn't look like Leyton and I are going to find our costumes in other people's trash."

"Wait." TJ stopped in front of the house next to theirs. "What about this stuff?"

Lying on the curb was a huge white cardboard tube, big enough for a boy to fit inside. Beside it was an old pillow with white stuffing leaking out of it, and an old dark yellow rain slicker.

"We can't make costumes out of this junk," said Wade.

"How do you know?" asked TJ. "We should take it home just in case."

Wade thought his little brother's

suggestion was silly, but he couldn't think of anything else to make costumes from, so they picked up the junk and headed home. Inside their house, they left the huge cardboard tube, leaking pillow, and old rain slicker by the front door, and went to have dinner.

Wade and TJ had a frozen pizza, and Leyton snuck off to eat his Brain Food. After dinner, TJ went to the den to watch TV. Wade planned to go to his room and study vocabulary because he needed to know lots of words if he wanted to be TOTALLY BEYOND EXCELLENT IN SCHOOL and get a scholarship to college. Leyton pulled on a pair of work gloves and took a shovel out of the broom closet. Ever since the winter before, when the boys had searched their house for the cat they'd never seen in the basement they didn't have, Leyton had been a Boy On A Mission.

"How is your project coming along?" Wade asked.

"Good," answered Leyton as he swung the shovel over his shoulder. "I should be finished soon."

"Well, I've told you this before," said Wade. "I think you're completely insane, but I admire your determination."

"Thank you," said Leyton.

Wade went upstairs to study vocabulary.

Leyton went downstairs . . . to dig a basement.

COULD
EVERYTHING
BE
WRONG?

The next morning, Daisy stopped by the Tardy Boys' house on the way to school.

"Did you find anything to make costumes out of?" she asked while she waited for the Tardy Boys to get their things.

"Just this junk." Leyton pointed at the

cardboard tube, leaky old pillow, and the dark yellow rain slicker lying on the floor.

"I hate to say it, but it's going to be hard to make costumes out of that," said Daisy.

"I know," said Wade. "And if we don't come up with costumes by tonight, we won't be able to enter the Halloween Costume Contest."

They started to walk to school. Waiting for them at the corner was their good friend Al-Ian Konspiracy. He was wearing his black Velostat Thought-Screen Helmet and football shoulder pads covered with aluminum foil.

"How come you're wearing your Halloween costume now?" asked TJ.

"I'm not," said Al-Ian. "This hat stops aliens from reading my mind and controlling my thoughts. The aluminum

foil on these shoulder pads deflects alien body heat sensor rays."

"Then what will your Halloween costume be?" asked Daisy.

"I won't be wearing a costume because I won't be going out on Halloween," Al-Ian said. "There are more alien abductions on Halloween than any other night of the year. It's the one night that aliens can walk among us unnoticed."

"It's also the one night of the year when we can get as much free candy as we can carry," Leyton reminded him.

"You think getting free candy is worth the risk of being kidnapped by aliens?" Al-Ian asked.

"Absolutely," said Leyton.

"Without a doubt," agreed Wade.

"Just because the aliens who kidnapped

your parents gave them pizza and let them watch TV doesn't mean all aliens are nice," Al-Ian warned. "Believe me, there are some really awful, nasty aliens out there and you wouldn't want to be kidnapped by them."

"Know what's strange?" Wade asked.

"More people use blue toothbrushes than red ones?" TJ guessed.

"No," said Wade.

"Giraffe tongues are so long they use them to clean their ears?" guessed Daisy.

"No," said Wade.

"The original name for the butterfly was the flutterby?" guessed Leyton.

"Did you make that up?" Al-Ian asked him.

"I'm not sure," answered Leyton. "I mean, it's true that butterflies sometimes flutter by, but no matter how I try, I can't deny that I sometimes lie."

"That's not what's strange," said Wade. "What's strange is that we walked all the way to school and Barton Slugg didn't attack us. And now we're at school and Mrs. Mandible isn't here screaming and Fibby isn't hiding behind her."

"That is strange," said Daisy. "But not as strange as the fact that it takes three thousand cows to supply the National Football League with enough leather for a year's supply of footballs."

By now the Tardy Boys and their friends had arrived at The School With No Name. As usual, Assistant Principal Snout was standing outside the front doors wearing blue latex gloves, yellow earplugs, and a white breathing mask. Some people might have thought this was a Halloween costume, but it wasn't. It was what the assistant principal wore every day. The assistant principal looked at his watch and frowned. "Late again. Why can't you ever be on time?"

Usually Leyton did not try to come up with answers to questions like this because he assumed his skull was empty. Even this morning, he didn't think he would have an answer because the billions of brand-new, teensy-weensy, itsy-bitsy, baby brain cells in his skull were not yet old enough to have ideas. So Leyton was caught completely by surprise when all those teensy-weensy, itsy-bitsy, baby brain cells suddenly began to jiggle and vibrate. *Boing!* An answer bubbled up into his mind.

"I know the answer!" he blurted.

Everyone stared at him in amazement.

"What if we *are* on time, and *you're* just early?" asked Leyton.

Assistant Principal Snout scowled and checked his watch. "No, according to my watch, you are fifteen minutes late."

"Then maybe your watch is fast," said Daisy.

Assistant Principal Snout blinked nervously. "No, that can't be. My watch is synchronized with the bells."

"Then the bells must be wrong," said Al-Ian.

By now, tiny beads of sweat were beginning to appear on Assistant Principal Snout's forehead. It had never occurred to him that the bells might be wrong. This was a very scary thought because he lived by the bells. They told him when to get up, when to dress, when to eat, when to yell at kids, and when to go to bed. (Sometimes Assistant Principal Snout stayed at school for weeks.)

"What if Leyton's right?" Wade asked. "What if the clocks and bells are all wrong? What if we've always been on time and everyone else has just been early?"

Sweat dripped down Assistant Principal Snout's forehead. His heart beat faster and his head throbbed. If the bells were wrong, then EVERYTHING WAS WRONG!

I have to speak to Janitor Shotput, he mumbled to himself. *She'll know. She's the one who sets the bells. If the bells are wrong, that's her fault, not mine. I can't be held responsible for things like that. I have too many other responsibilities. Like yelling at kids and putting them in detention and making sure they wash their hands.*

"Uh, Assistant Principal Snout?" said Wade.

But Assistant Principal Snout was busy mumbling to himself. *So if they ask who's at fault, I'll say Janitor Shotput. If they ask where I was, I'll say I wasn't there. I didn't see or hear anything. I was only an innocent bystander. It wasn't me. It was probably someone who just looked like me. That's it! It was identity theft! Someone pretending to be me is running around setting the clocks wrong!*

No matter how the Tardy Boys and their friends tried, they couldn't get Assistant Principal Snout's attention. Finally, they gave up and went into school.

ON
A
ROLL

A few moments later, the Tardy Boys and their friends (but not TJ because he went to the elementary school) entered Ms. Fitt's classroom. Ms. Fitt had red hair that hung down past her shoulders in ringlets. She liked to wear big earrings and colorful clothes. Today she was wearing a long, baggy red sweater that hung down past her knees. The sleeves hung way past her hands. On her feet were a pair of enormous old boots.

When the Tardy Boys got to class, they saw Barton Slugg, their WORST ARCH-ENEMY EVER. But this was not the OLD Barton Slugg. This was the NEW Barton Slugg. It was true that he still had buck teeth and brown hair that fell into his eyes. And he was still the biggest slimeball ever. But he no longer left a trail of slime wherever he walked. Nor did his feet give off an odor so strong that it made your eyes tear and burned the insides of your nostrils. WHY? Because thanks to DR. YANKUM'S TOE FLOSS, Barton Slugg no longer had the world's stinkiest toe cheese.

In fact, Barton Slugg no longer had any toe cheese whatsoever.

While the Tardy Boys and their friends sat down, Barton raised his hand.

"Yes, Barton?" said Ms. Fitt.

"Why are you wearing clothes that don't fit?" Barton asked.

"I'm wearing my Halloween costume in school because I won't have time to go home after school and change for the costume contest," Ms. Fitt answered.

"So for a Halloween costume you're wearing clothes that don't fit?" Barton asked, clearly puzzled.

"Yes, because I'm Ms. Fitt," she said.

Fibby Mandible raised her hand. Fibby was not the Tardy Boys' WORST ARCH-ENEMY EVER, but she came close. Fibby had streaked blonde hair and a freckled nose and so many clothes that she never wore the same thing twice. Fibby's

mother, Ulna, was certain that Fibby was allergic to milk, nuts, chocolate, vegetables, berries, dust, pollen, smoke, math, and gym, but she probably wasn't. The one thing Fibby definitely was allergic to was animal fur, but thanks to Dr. Crock and his amazing Herbal Sodium Pentothal, this was no longer a problem.

But Sodium Pentothal was also known as truth serum, and it had one unexpected side effect: It made Fibby tell the truth.

"Yes, Fibby," said Ms. Fitt.

Fibby pointed at a large bright red plastic barrel on wheels. On top of the barrel was a sign that said CANDY CHARITY. "What's that for?" she asked.

"Thank you for reminding me, Fibby," said Ms. Fitt. "This year, we are running a candy charity for poor children. We are hoping that after the King of Candy

Contest each of you will donate some of your candy to the charity."

All around the room, kids began to mutter. No one liked the idea of giving away any of their Halloween candy.

"I'm not giving my candy to some stupid charity," said Fibby. "I'm keeping every single piece for myself."

Al-Ian raised his hand.

"Yes?" said Ms. Fitt.

"What's the small print at the bottom of the sign say?" Al-Ian asked.

"Oh, I didn't notice that before." Ms. Fitt bent down next to the bright red plastic barrel. "It says, 'This contest is sponsored by the American Dental Association.'" Ms. Fitt turned to the class. "Isn't that nice? The American Dental Association wants to make sure that all children get candy at Halloween. Anyway, today we're going to begin our unit on analyzing poetry. Does everyone know what that means?"

No one answered.

"To analyze a poem means to figure out what it's really about," Ms. Fitt explained.

Al-Ian raised his hand. "Isn't a poem about what the words say it's about?"

"Excellent question," said Ms. Fitt. "And the answer is, no. Sometimes a poem is about something completely different than what you think."

"How can that be?" asked Daisy.

"Because poets use similes and metaphors," Ms. Fitt explained. "A simile is when two unlike things are compared. For instance, if I were to say 'You are as pretty as a rose,' I wouldn't mean that you look like a rose. I'd mean that like most roses, you are very pretty. A metaphor is like a simile, only different. Metaphors generally don't use the words *like* or *as*. Here's an example: 'Still waters run deep.' What do you think that means, Al-Ian?"

"Uh, that deep down there's still water, but it's running?" Al-Ian said.

"If it's still, it can't run, stupid," Barton muttered.

"Barton, it's not nice to call people stupid even when they appear to be," Ms. Fitt gently scolded him, then returned to Al-Ian. "It means that sometimes when someone appears calm and doesn't react quickly, they may actually be thinking very hard about something."

"But you didn't say anything about a person who was calm or thinking," Al-Ian said. "You were talking about water."

"That's why it's a metaphor," Ms. Fitt

said. "You have to look past the literal meaning. Here's another example. Have you ever heard someone say you have to grab the bull by the horns?"

A few kids nodded.

"What do you think that means?"

No one raised their hands.

"Come on," Ms. Fitt urged them. "Take a guess. Leyton, what do you think it means?"

Leyton waited to see if the billions of brand-new, teensy-weensy, itsy-bitsy, baby brain cells in his skull were ready to have another idea, but because they were still babies, they were napping and didn't hear Ms. Fitt's question. So Leyton could only guess. "Uh, that you have to grab it by the horns because it's hard to reach the ears?"

"Not quite," said Ms. Fitt. "Anyone else?"

Barton raised his hand. "That you have to grab it by the horns because otherwise it'll gore you?"

"That's a little closer, but still not there," said Ms. Fitt. "Anyone else?"

No one raised their hand.

"Suppose I told you that it meant that the best way to deal with a problem is to face it and fix it and not run away from it?" Ms. Fitt asked.

"You mean, the bull is the problem?" asked Daisy.

"Exactly," said Ms. Fitt. "Now here's your homework assignment. I want each of you to find a poem and analyze it. You can either write your analysis as an essay or present it verbally in class. Or, if you'd like, you can write your own poem using similes and metaphors."

And then the bell rang.

The Tardy Boys and their friends went out into the hall.

"Was that amazing or what?" Al-Ian said excitedly. "Who knew you could write one thing and mean something else completely? I mean, they're all around us and we don't even know it."

"What's all around us?" Wade asked.

"Metaphors and similes." Al-Ian pointed at a door. "You see how the sign over that door says EXIT? But it's also an entrance!"

"Yes," Wade began to say, "but I'm not sure that's what Ms. Fitt —"

"And you know how sometimes people say something is really sick when it's really cool?" Al-Ian went on. "So sometimes sick is cool, but sometimes sick is sick."

"That's true, Al-Ian," said Daisy, "but —"

"And here's another one!" Al-Ian said. "My sister's always talking about hot guys. But are they really hot? No! They're usually pretty cool! And it's the same with *bad*. Sometimes when something is really good you say it's bad. But other times it really is bad."

"You're really on a roll, Al-Ian," said Leyton.

"Exactly!" cried Al-Ian. "But am I *actually* on a roll? Of course not! I'm actually walking down the hall in school, not lying on some big hamburger bun. And then there's —"

Al-Ian went on and on. There was no stopping him.

GUT-WRENCHING
BULLDOZER
HORNS

School was over and it was time to go home. As the Tardy Boys and their friends headed for the main entrance that was also an exit, Assistant Principal Snout was waiting for them.

"Aha!" he said. "Wait right here." He took out his walkie-talkie. "Silver-medal-winning Janitor Shotput, please come to the front entrance immediately."

Faster than you could say stopwatch backward, Olga Shotput arrived. Olga was a large woman with short hair and muscular arms. Around her neck the silver top of a tuna fish can hung on a red, white, and blue ribbon. She clicked her heels together and saluted. "At your service, Assistant Principal Snout."

"Olga," Principal Snout said. "Tell these students how you know that the bells are set to the correct time."

Olga Shotput, the silver-medal-winning janitor, blinked. Then she bit her lip. Then she frowned and scratched her chin. "I don't."

Assistant Principal Snout turned pale. "What do you mean, you don't?"

"I mean, I just set the bells to my watch," said Olga.

"And what do you set your watch to?" asked Assistant Principal Snout.

"I haven't set my watch since I came here many years ago to participate in the Spring Olympics," said Olga.

"But there are no Spring Olympics," said Assistant Principal Snout.

"You're telling me?" Olga groaned. "Believe me, I know."

Assistant Principal Snout broke into a light sweat. "So you *never* adjust the clocks?"

"Only for Moonlight Savings Time," Olga answered.

"Oh, my gosh!" Assistant Principal Snout started to tremble. "This is terrible! All the clocks and bells in school are set to a watch that could be wrong! There's no way to tell who's on time and who's late!"

An instant later, he dashed down the hall and into his office.

"That man needs a vacation," Olga muttered.

"When was the last time he took one?" asked Daisy.

"Never," said the silver-medal-winning janitor. "I've been at this school for twelve years and he's never left."

"What about summer?" asked Leyton.

"Summer school," answered Olga.

"What about Christmas and Easter?" asked Wade.

"He stays," said Olga. "He says he doesn't, but I find the empty pizza boxes in the garbage."

"Wow, that's crazy," said Al-Ian.

"Yes, but I also think he will win a gold medal in attendance someday," Olga said, and walked away.

The Tardy Boys and their friends left school and started toward home. The Halloween Costume Contest was that evening. When they got home, they passed the big cardboard tube, leaky pillow, and old yellow rain slicker in the hall and went into the kitchen.

"What are we gonna do about costumes?" Leyton asked Wade as they sat down at the kitchen table.

Wade propped his chin in his hands and shook his head sadly. "Not a clue."

"Think we should skip the contest?" Leyton asked.

"Forget the contest," said Wade. "Tomorrow's Halloween. How are we going to trick-or-treat if we don't have costumes? My hypothesis has two parts. The first part is that the houses with the best decorations give the most candy. The

second part is that the kids with the best costumes get the most candy."

"So if we don't have good costumes we won't get a lot of candy," Leyton realized.

"Exactly," said Wade miserably.

Leyton felt his guts wrench. He wasn't sure where his guts were, or how there could be a wrench in them, but just the same, he felt bad for his brother. It was true that Wade sometimes treated him like a dummy, but that was before the billions of brand-new, teensy-weensy, itsy-bitsy, baby brain cells began to grow in Leyton's skull.

TJ came into the kitchen with the Extra-Large Mens Jockey-Style Undergarment stretched over his head. "How do I look?" he asked.

"Like an Atomic Wedgie," said Leyton.

"Really?!" TJ cried happily.

"Yup." Wade nodded sadly.

The smile disappeared from TJ's face. "Are you guys freaked because you still don't have any ideas for costumes?"

Wade and Leyton nodded.

"Bummer," said TJ.

"Mega-Bummer," Wade agreed unhappily.

Leyton hated to see Wade suffering from Mega-Bummerdom. He hated feeling the wrench in his gut even though it probably felt better than how a sledgehammer in his gut would feel. And definitely better than a bulldozer. And that made him wonder if people ever grabbed bulldozers by the horns. And did bulldozers even have horns? Or did they just have those little beep-beep thingies for backing up?

And that made him wonder about their costume problem. Wade couldn't think of any costumes for them, and Wade was really smart. Usually, if Wade couldn't think of an answer to a problem, Leyton assumed that he couldn't think of one, either. But that was then and this was now, and growing in his skull were billions of brand-new, teensy-weensy, itsy-bitsy, baby brain cells. Why weren't they doing their job? He'd been feeding them Brain Food and taking care of them for months. Was this how they showed their gratitude? By lying around in his skull and napping and not taking the bull by the horns?

Hey, brand-new, teensy-weensy, itsy-bitsy, baby brain cells! Leyton shouted in his head. *It's time to take the bull by the horns.*

And that's exactly what those brand-new, teensy-weensy, itsy-bitsy, baby brain cells did.

TREE HUGGER

A few hours later, students began to gather in the gym of The School With No Name for the Halloween Costume Contest. As usual, Assistant Principal Snout stood by the entrance and watched who entered. When he saw the Tardy Boys and their friends, he started to check his watch.

"You're lucky," he said to them.

"Why?" asked Wade.

"Because you might be late, but I can't prove it," said the assistant principal. "So go inside. The competition is about to begin."

"Why do we always have to have all these contests?" asked Daisy, who was dressed as a windmill.

"Competition is good for you," said Assistant Principal Snout.

"Why?" asked Daisy.

"Because it toughens you up," said Assistant Principal Snout.

"Why do we need to be tough?" asked Daisy.

"Because school prepares you for the world, and the world is a dangerous place filled with germ-ridden children and screaming mothers and poor oral hygiene," said Assistant Principal Snout.

"I really don't see how competition could either toughen you up or prepare you for those things," said Daisy.

Assistant Principal Snout started to look annoyed. "Well, it can, okay? Why can't you just accept that? All that peace and love hippie garbage is over, okay? Life is hard and it's scary out there. Why do you think I never leave school? And besides, no one's making you compete."

"I'm not here to compete," said Daisy. "I'm here to inform people about alternative sources of energy."

"Yeah, well, go hug a tree," Assistant Principal Snout grumbled, and waved them inside.

Inside, the gym was crowded with kids wearing costumes. Way down at the far end was a panel of judges. One by one, kids went up and were judged by the panel while the crowd watched. When a kid went up dressed as a giant lightbulb, Daisy gasped, "It's Barton!"

"What's so great about being a giant lightbulb?" TJ asked.

"Don't ask me," said Wade.

From the frowns and scowls on their faces, it appeared that the contest judges were also puzzled. But then Barton nodded at the silver-medal-winning janitor, Olga Shotput, who flicked off the light switches near the door.

The gym became dark.

Barton's lightbulb costume started glowing like a regular lightbulb. Then it became pink, then green, then yellow. The crowd "oohed" and "ahhed." But Barton wasn't finished. Next the lightbulb costume became striped orange and red, then ringed with blue and green, then all yellow with pink polka dots. The crowd murmured in wonder and then began to clap.

"That's amazing!" gasped Daisy.

"And it's not plugged into electricity," added Al-Ian. "I don't see any cords."

This was true. While Barton might have been carrying batteries that helped his costume light up, it wasn't as if he needed an electric wire and an outlet. There was no doubt in the Tardy Boys' minds that Barton would win the Halloween Costume Contest. No one else would even come close.

GLOWOLOGY

The contest ended and Barton was declared the winner. He bowed to the crowd. The Tardy Boys and their friends joined in the applause.

"You have to admit that it's an amazing costume," said Daisy.

"Yeah, and that's really bad news," said Wade.

"Why?" asked Daisy.

"Because my hypothesis states that the better your costume, the more candy you'll collect," Wade said. "And if I'm right, then Barton will win the King of Candy Contest, too. And if I'm wrong, then my hypothesis is wrong. So either way, I lose."

"Winning isn't everything," said Daisy.

"Ahem," Al-Ian cleared his throat. "Look who's coming."

It was Barton in his lightbulb costume. The Tardy Boys braced themselves, expecting Barton to act like a big-shot winner. But before Barton could speak, Daisy said, "That is the best costume I've ever seen."

Instead of saying something mean or nasty, Barton smiled and said, "You really think so?"

"Yes," said Daisy. "It's just amazing."

"Thank you," Barton said. "And I really like your windmill costume. It's too bad it doesn't produce real electricity because then we'd be a perfect match. You could supply me with electricity, and I could provide you with light."

The Tardy Boys didn't know what to think. It actually seemed like Barton was being nice. Suddenly, Mrs. Peduncle appeared through the crowd wearing a fringed deerskin jacket and slacks.

"What are you doing here, Mom?" Daisy asked.

"You haven't forgotten about your weekly aromatherapy appointment, have you?" Mrs. Peduncle asked.

"Oh, my gosh!" Daisy gasped. She and her mom hurried out of the gym, leaving the Tardy Boys and Al-Ian with Barton.

No sooner was Daisy gone, than Barton glared at Wade and Leyton and his lips curled into a sneer. "What are you guys supposed to be in those stupid costumes?"

Wade was wearing the big white cardboard tube. He'd cut holes on the sides so his arms could stick out, and a circle in the front for his face. On the top of the tube, he'd glued the white stuffing from the inside of the pillow. Leyton was wearing the old dark yellow rain slicker.

"I'm a Q-tip," said Wade.

Barton rolled his eyes in disbelief and looked at Leyton. "What about you?"

"Earwax," said Leyton.

"You guys are total losers," said Barton.

"So, how does your costume work?" Al-Ian asked him.

Barton's face hardened. "That's a secret."

"It must run on batteries, right?" said Wade.

"It takes a lot more than batteries," said Barton.

"Where'd you get it?" asked Leyton.

"It was created for me by my aunt," Barton said. "She's the world's foremost glowologist."

"What's a glowologist?" asked Al-Ian.

Barton smirked as if the answer should have been obvious. "A glowologist is someone who makes things glow, dimwit."

"Does she work with bunnies?" TJ asked.

"Why do you ask?" said Barton.

"Because last night I thought I saw a green glow-in-the-dark bunny," said TJ.

Al-Ian turned pale. "Are you serious?"

TJ nodded. "I thought I saw it behind a bush."

"When Leyton and I went behind the bush to look, we didn't find anything," Wade said.

"It might have been hiding," said TJ.

Al-Ian began to tremble. "This is bad. Really bad. Listen, TJ, I need you to think really hard. I know you said it was a glow-in-the-dark bunny, but was it also a cuddly bunny?"

TJ rubbed his chin and thought for a moment. Then he nodded. "Yes, I'd say it was also cuddly."

Al-Ian's trembles became shakes. "Oh, this is horrible! Just terrible!"

"Why?" asked Leyton.

"Because there's only one alien species in the entire universe that fits that description," Al-Ian said. "And they're the Cuddly Glowbunnies from Planet Neon in the Glowstick Galaxy!"

CUDDLY GLOWBUNNIES

"So?" said Barton.

"The Cuddly Glowbunnies are the fiercest, meanest, most sinister aliens in the entire universe!" Al-Ian gasped. "They take over every planet they want. No one has ever been able to stop them. They are feared and dreaded everywhere. If they're here, it's because they want the Earth."

"Are you saying that the most feared

aliens in the entire universe are called Cuddly Glowbunnies?" Wade asked with a smile.

"Yes! Exactly!" said Al-Ian.

"Know what, Al-Ian?" Barton said with a smirk. "There's only one bunny around here that anyone has to worry about, and that's you. Because you're a psycho-bunny."

"How can you say that after the orange-striped space cat took Tinker Bell back to Planet Hiss?" Al-Ian asked.

Barton's eyes began to fill with tears. "Don't you ever mention Tinker Bell's name again!" he cried, and then hurried off.

"Attention, everyone," Assistant Principal Snout announced over the loudspeaker. "We will now give out the consolation prizes."

"What's a consolation prize?" asked TJ.

"That's what they give losers so they don't feel as bad about not winning," said Wade.

"You mean, you have to lose to win one?" asked Al-Ian.

"Right," said Wade.

"Aha!" said Al-Ian. "Another example of something that means something else!"

Assistant Principal Snout held up a bag of candy corn. "The first consolation prize goes to the most environmentally friendly costume. That would be Daisy Peduncle for her windmill outfit. Is Daisy here?"

"She had to go to her aromatherapy appointment," said Wade.

"Really? Then I guess I'll just keep this." Assistant Principal Snout slid the bag of candy corn into his pocket. "The next prize is for the most creative costumes made from the most unlikely junk. And that one goes to Wade and Leyton Tardy for their Q-tip and earwax combination."

Wade got the prize and then returned to his brothers and Al-Ian with a dull brown grocery bag.

"What'd you win?" TJ asked excitedly.

"A bunch of cheap plastic Halloween masks," Wade said, opening the bag to show them.

"What are you going to do with them?" asked Al-Ian.

"Don't know." Wade shrugged.

"Maybe Assistant Principal Snout will trade them for Daisy's candy corn," said TJ. "After all, Daisy doesn't eat candy."

"Good idea," said Wade. But when they looked at Assistant Principal Snout, he had taken the bag out of his pocket and was eating the candy corn himself.

"Oh, well, forget that idea," said TJ.

Now that the Halloween Costume Contest was over, the Tardy Boys and Al-Ian started to walk home. It was getting dark and the streetlights had just gone on. Al-Ian swiveled his head back and forth nervously.

"What's wrong?" Wade asked him.

"I'm looking for Cuddly Glowbunnies," Al-Ian answered. "If they're really here, then Planet Earth is in big, big trouble."

"Are you sure, Al-Ian?" asked Wade. "The Cuddly Glowbunnies don't *sound* like the meanest, fiercest, cruelest aliens in the whole universe."

"That's the whole point!" said Al-Ian. "Don't you understand? They only *call* themselves the Cuddly Glowbunnies. But that's not what the words really mean."

"I'm starting to think that maybe you're

taking this simile and metaphor thing a little too far," said Wade. "I mean, cuddly pretty much means cuddly, and bunnies are basically bunnies."

Al-Ian shook his head. "You're totally wrong, Wade. But I know you won't believe me until you see one for yourself. Only, by then, it will be too late."

They reached the street where Al-Ian lived. "I'll see you guys in the morning," Al-Ian said. "That is, *if* we're all still here."

After Al-Ian left, the Tardy Boys continued toward their own house.

"So what do you think about the Cuddly Glowbunnies?" Wade asked.

"Sounds a little weird to me," said TJ. "Even though I know I saw a glow-in-the-dark bunny last night, it sure didn't look like the meanest, fiercest, cruelest alien in the whole universe."

"Yeah," Wade agreed. "What do you think, Leyton?"

Leyton was just about to answer when he thought he saw something pink out of the corner of his eye. He twisted around and saw what looked like a pink glow-in-the-dark bunny scamper behind a tree. But had he really seen it? Or had he just imagined it?

"Leyton?" Wade said. "I asked what you thought about the Cuddly Glowbunnies."

"Uh, I need to think about it some more," said Leyton.

ANOTHER POEM

The next day was Halloween.

"I'm going to win the King of Candy Contest by collecting more candy than anyone," Barton bragged in the school hallway.

"Or buying it," Leyton said.

"No way," said Barton. "Anyone can buy a lot of candy and win the contest, but that doesn't prove anything. I'm going to win by collecting more candy because people always want to give the most candy to the kid with the best costume."

"That's my hypothesis," said Wade.

Barton looked around. "Where?"

"You can't see a hypothesis," Wade said.

"Why not?" asked Barton.

"They're invisible until you write them down," said Al-Ian.

Barton frowned and looked at Al-Ian. "Is this one of your psycho-bunny nutcase alien ideas?"

"It's science," said Wade.

Barton smirked. "Well, it may be *your* hypothesis, but it's going to be *my* candy."

Then he turned and strutted away down the hall.

"I wish my hypothesis was wrong," Wade said with a sigh.

"Hey, guys." Daisy came toward them. "Look what I found in my locker this morning." She handed Wade a folded piece of lined paper. Wade unfolded it and read the note out loud:

To Daisy, another poem from your Secret Admirer

Your Halloween costume showed such flair
You and I would make a wonderful pair.
Together there is nothing we couldn't do
We could conquer the world if we wanted to.
Tear down great buildings; turn day to night.
When I think of you, everything feels right.
You are the only girl I adore.
So pritty, so smart; who could ask for more?
I wish I could tell you who I am.
Maybe someday you will understand
And the world will be ours once and for all.
And I will be your boyfriend, even though I'm not tall.

"Whoever is writing these poems must really like you," said Wade.

"And isn't very tall," added Leyton.

"How many poems like this have you gotten?" asked Al-Ian.

"Two so far," said Daisy. "I always find them in my locker."

"And *pretty* is always spelled wrong," added Wade.

"Do you think I could get copies of these poems?" Al-Ian asked.

"Sure, but why would you want them?" Daisy asked.

"I'd like to analyze them," Al-Ian said.

"Okay," Daisy said. "I'll make copies after school. You can pick them up tonight when you stop at my house to trick-or-treat."

"Thanks, but I won't be trick-or-treating tonight," said Al-Ian.

"Then maybe Wade and Leyton will pick up the poems when they come by," Daisy said.

Wade and Leyton shared an uncomfortable glance.

"We weren't planning on stopping at your house tonight, Daisy," Wade said. "No offense or anything, but organic carrots don't really count as candy."

"But they're good for you," said Daisy.

"Yes," said Leyton. "That's the problem."

NOT ON THE MAP

At five P.M. the Tardy Boys put on their Halloween costumes, grabbed old pillowcases, and began collecting candy as fast as they could, following the map they'd planned out earlier in the week. Almost every house with good Halloween decorations had lots of treats, but the treats weren't always the ones the Tardy Boys expected.

"A pack of cheese and crackers?" Wade said unhappily when he and his brothers stopped in the street to see what they'd collected.

"I got a bag of peanuts in the shell," said TJ.

"Three packs of sugar-free gum," complained Leyton.

"I don't get it," said Wade. "Don't they know we want candy?"

"Hello, boys," someone said. The Tardy Boys looked up from their pillowcases. Coming toward them was a huge, muscular man. His arms were as round as car tires and his legs were as thick as tree trunks. He had scars on his jaw and permanently swollen eyes and a crooked nose that looked like it had been broken at least twenty times. He was wearing black nylon shorts and a hooded black sweatshirt and was walking a small old pug dog.

"Hi, Mr. Roy," said the Tardy Boys. They all bent down to pet the dog, whose name was Wheezy.

"How's the trick-or-treating this year?" said Mr. Roy.

"Not so good," said Wade. "Instead of candy, a lot of houses are giving us junk like packets of cheese and crackers, and peanuts in shells, and sugar-free gum."

"I bet it's because of that newspaper article last week," said Mr. Roy. "It was all about giving healthy Halloween treats."

"That's ridiculous!" said TJ.

"That's what I thought," said Mr. Roy. "I mean, why bother having Halloween if you can't get enough candy to make you totally sick?"

"Exactly," agreed the Tardy Boys.

Even though he was standing on his stiff little legs, Wheezy's head dipped and he began to wheeze softly and steadily. "Uh-oh, look who fell asleep." Mr. Roy bent down and gently lifted the little dog into his huge arms. "I guess the little guy got tired out. I better take him home. See you later, boys. Hope you find some good candy."

The Tardy Boys headed toward the next house on their map.

"Who ever heard of healthy Halloween treats?" Wade grumbled as they walked through the dark.

"It's like the world's gone crazy," said Leyton.

Just then, TJ stopped and pointed at a small, old white house with peeling paint and broken shutters. "What about that house?"

"Forget it," Wade said. "It's not on the map."

"They can't even afford a new paint job," said Leyton.

"But look," said TJ as a mother came down the front walk with two little kids — a boy dressed in black like a magician and a girl dressed in a pink dress like a princess. They stopped at the curb and opened the orange-and-black Halloween bags they'd just gotten. Both kids grinned broadly as if they were happy with what was inside the bags.

"Those bags look pretty full," said Leyton.

"Maybe it's worth a try," said TJ.

"Okay, but only for the sake of the scientific method," said Wade.

They went up to the front door of the small white house and rang the bell. A thin old woman with long gray hair and yellow teeth came to the door. Just inside the door was a big bin with fat orange-and-black bags filled with candy. The old woman squinted at the Tardy Boys and her face wrinkled. She looked a little scary, but she had a kind smile. "My, my, my, what are you supposed to be?"

"I'm an Atomic Wedgie," said TJ.

The old woman clasped her wrinkled hands together. "Oh, I should have guessed that! I'm sorry, but I've misplaced my glasses and it's hard for me to see." Then she squinted at Wade and Leyton. "And you two?"

"I'm a Q-tip," Wade said.

The old woman smiled. "How clever!" Then she squinted at Leyton. Suddenly, her jaw fell open and she laughed. "And you're earwax! Oh, that's funny! Well, here you are." She gave each of them a bulging Halloween bag of candy. The Tardy Boys thanked her and left. They were crossing the street to another house when TJ suddenly shouted, "Watch out!"

Wade and Leyton spun around. A pair of headlights was barreling toward them!

BIG
RED
WAX
LIPS

The Tardy Boys dove out of the way, spilling some of their candy on the ground. A split-second later a big red Hummer raced past and skidded to a stop. The doors swung open, and Fibby Mandible and three other kids jumped out and raced to the closest houses to trick-or-treat. As soon as they were finished, they raced back to the Hummer and jumped back in.

Screech! The Hummer took off for the next set of houses.

"Know who that was?" Wade said.

"Fibby?" guessed TJ.

"Right," said Wade.

"But who were the other kids?" TJ asked.

"Normally I'd say they were her friends," said Wade. "Only, Fibby doesn't have three friends. So that can only mean one thing. They're hired guns!"

"What's a hired gun?" TJ asked.

As soon as TJ asked that question, Leyton felt a funny sensation inside his skull. Now that they were old enough to start having ideas, the billions of brand-new, teensy-weensy, itsy-bitsy, baby brain cells sprang into action. *Boing!* They instantly provided the answer. "A hired gun is a gunfighter or professional killer who is hired to kill someone," he said.

"Only in this case, those kids aren't literally hired to kill. Fibby hired them to trick-or-treat. So the phrase *hired gun* is being used as a metaphor."

Wade stared at his brother in amazement. "That's *exactly* right."

Leyton beamed proudly. It felt good when his brother complimented him on his newly grown brains. "And the reason Fibby's got hired guns to help her trick-or-treat is that she wants to win the King of Candy Contest."

"But that's cheating," said TJ.

"Fibby always cheats," said Wade. "We better get the candy that spilled and keep going before time runs out."

TJ bent down and picked up the bulging orange-and-black candy bag the old lady had just given him. "Hey, what is this stuff?"

Inside the bags were candies the boys had never seen before: little wax bottles filled with flavored syrups, thin white candy cigarettes with red tips, big red wax lips, and candy dots on strips of white paper.

"Looks like old-fashioned candy," said Wade.

"What a waste," TJ grumbled.

"Maybe not," said Wade. "We might not like the candy, but at least there's a lot of it, and that's gonna help us in the King of Candy Contest."

The boys headed down the street toward the next house on Wade's map. By now, it was almost six thirty and Leyton's stomach was growling. "It's past dinnertime," he complained. "I'm hungry."

"Don't eat any candy," Wade warned. "You'll need it for the contest."

"Forget it," said Leyton. "Between Barton and his amazing costume, and Fibby and her hired guns, we're never gonna win the contest."

"We can't give up," said Wade.

Leyton didn't want to give up, but the billions of brand-new, teensy-weensy, itsy-bitsy, baby brain cells in his skull were hungry and crying out to be fed. As they walked toward the next house, Leyton fell behind. When his brothers weren't looking, he reached into his pillowcase for something big and quickly shoved it into his mouth. He started to chew.

At first, it felt kind of waxy and he wasn't sure he was going to like it.

But then, it started to taste sweet and tangy and fruity!

Not like anything he'd ever tasted before!

And no matter how much he chewed, the taste was still there!

"What are you doing?" Wade asked.

Leyton looked up. Wade was standing in front of him with his arms crossed. Leyton couldn't answer because his mouth was filled with the delicious, fruity, waxy candy.

"What's the big bulge in your cheek?" his brother demanded.

"Nuffing," Leyton said with his mouth full.

"You're eating candy," Wade said. "How do you expect to win the King of Candy Contest?"

"I toll you I wuff fungry," Leyton said. "Befides thiff is rearry goob."

"Which candy is it?" TJ asked, eagerly reaching into his bag.

"Not you, too," muttered Wade.

"Dude, I'm hungry," said TJ. "It's unnatural to collect all this candy and not eat any of it."

"It's big, wed, and waxy," said Leyton.

TJ pulled out something that looked like big red wax lips. He made a face. "Looks totally gross."

By now, Leyton had chewed the candy down to a manageable size and could speak more clearly. "You can't judge a book by its cover."

TJ looked down at the big red wax lips in his hand. "This isn't a book."

"It's a metaphor," said Leyton.

"Actually, it's more like an aphorism," said Wade.

"Whatever," said Leyton. "Listen, TJ, if you don't want those wax lips, can I have them?"

TJ held the big red wax lips to his nose and sniffed. He took a small bite. "Hey, this is good!" He stuffed the rest into his mouth.

Wade watched as his brothers chewed happily on their wax lips. His stomach grumbled and he felt hungry, too. Was it really worth saving every piece of candy for the King of Candy Contest? Especially when Barton Slugg had such a fantastic costume and Fibby Mandible had hired guns? He reached into his pillowcase, pulled out the wax lips, and ate them.

Like Leyton and TJ, he wasn't sure at first. But the more he chewed, the better the candy seemed to get!

"Forget about the next house on the map," said TJ. "Let's go back to the old lady and get more wax lips."

"We can't go back," said Wade. "She'll recognize us."

Leyton knew that this was true. Once you'd been to a house trick-or-treating, you couldn't go back without risking being yelled at. Leyton didn't want to get yelled at, but he sure wanted more big red wax lips. The billions of brand-new, teensy-weensy, itsy-bitsy, baby brain cells growing in his skull started to wiggle.

The old lady had said she'd misplaced her glasses.

The billions of brand-new, teensy-weensy, itsy-bitsy, baby brain cells growing in his skull started to jiggle.

She had a hard time seeing.

Boing! Once again an idea popped into Leyton's head.

BETTER
THAN
NUTRICAT
DELUXE

A few moments later, the Tardy Boys were back at their house gathering up old clothes and the cheap plastic Halloween masks Wade and Leyton had won at the Halloween Costume Contest. Suddenly, there was a knock on the door.

"Who do you think that is?" TJ asked.

"Must be trick-or-treaters," said Wade.

"Do we have anything to give them?" Leyton asked.

"A pack of crackers and cheese and some sugarless gum," said TJ.

"Okay, go give it to them," Wade said.

TJ went to the front door. But when he came back, Al-Ian was with him. He was wearing his Velostat Thought-Screen Helmet and foil-covered shoulder pads.

"I thought you weren't going out tonight," Wade said.

"I wasn't," said Al-Ian, "but it got a little stuffy in my house and I decided to take a walk and get some fresh air. I saw the lights on in your house, so I decided to knock. How come you're not out trick-or-treating?"

Wade explained how they'd just come back to get spare costumes and about Leyton's plan to get more big red wax lips.

"Wax lips?" Al-Ian made a sour face.

"Don't knock it if you haven't tried it," said Leyton.

"Maybe you're right," said Al-Ian. "I guess I'll have to try one."

"You'll need a costume," said TJ.

Wade looked at Al-Ian's Velostat Thought-Screen Helmet and foil-covered shoulder pads. "I don't think that'll be a problem."

So Al-Ian went back with the Tardy Boys to the old lady's house. Wearing different combinations of masks and clothes, they went up to the old lady's door again and again until each of them had more than a dozen wax lips. By then it was eight o'clock — time to stop trick-or-treating and go home.

"That was great!" TJ said as he lugged his heavy pillowcase full of candy down the sidewalk. His cheeks bulged as he chewed on another wax lip.

"Yeah," agreed Leyton, "not only did we get more wax lips, but so much other candy that we may actually have a chance to win the King of Candy Contest."

"These things taste really good," Al-Ian said as he chewed on a pair of wax lips.

But Wade remained quiet.

"Is something wrong?" TJ asked.

"Maybe it wasn't right to take all that candy from the old lady," Wade said.

"But you saw how much she had in that bin," said Leyton. "Enough for tons more kids. I'll bet she'll have so much left over there'll be enough for next year."

"But that doesn't make it right to be greedy," argued Wade.

"You think we should bring it back?" asked Al-Ian.

"I don't know." Wade looked at his brother. "What do you think, Leyton?"

"Wow," said Leyton.

"Wow, what?" said Wade.

"You actually asked my opinion!" Leyton gasped. "Instead of just assuming I'd have no opinion because my skull has room for monkeys to swing in trees."

Wade blinked with astonishment. "You're right."

"And a little while ago, you said I was right when I told TJ what a hired gun was," Leyton reminded him.

"That's true," said Wade.

"You know what that means?" Leyton asked.

"That there may actually be a brain inside your skull," Wade realized.

"Yes!" Leyton cried. "And since you

asked me what I think we should do with the old lady's candy, here's my answer — I think . . . we should give it to charity. But only *after* the contest tomorrow."

Wade gazed at his brother in awe. "That's a fantastic idea!"

Leyton grinned happily. Wade had actually called his idea fantastic!

"This was the best Halloween ever," TJ exclaimed as they walked home through the dark.

"Thanks to Leyton's brilliant idea." Wade patted his brother on the shoulder.

Leyton beamed proudly. He'd never imagined it could feel this good to have a skull filled with billions of brand-new, teensy-weensy, itsy-bitsy, baby brain cells. It was better than almost anything else. Better than cartoons. Better than

Fluffernutter-in-a-jar. Better than wax lips. Even better than Nutricat Deluxe with mustard and soy sauce!

Suddenly, Wade saw something light blue out of the corner of his eye. He grabbed Leyton's arm. Leyton spun around and saw what his brother saw — hopping across a lawn toward them was . . . a real, nose-twitching, floppy-eared, light blue, glow-in-the-dark bunny!

Al-Ian dropped his pillowcase full of candy and screamed at the top of his lungs. "Run for your life!"

THE
TERRIBLE
TRUTH

The Tardy Boys dropped their bags and ran. But no matter how hard they ran, they couldn't catch up to Al-Ian. Wade had never seen their friend run this fast before. Al-Ian ran so fast that the Tardy Boys didn't have time to catch their breath. They didn't have time to think about what was going on.

Al-Ian ran straight to the Tardy Boys'

house, since that was the closest. "Lock the doors!" he cried once they were all inside.

The Tardy Boys ran around locking doors.

"Shut the windows!" Al-Ian shouted.

The Tardy Boys ran around shutting windows.

"Pull the shades!" Al-Ian yelled, and the Tardy Boys pulled the shades.

"Barricade the front door!" Al-Ian shouted, and started pushing a chest of drawers in front of the door.

"Wait a minute," Wade said.

"No!" Al-Ian gasped. "There's no time! We have to protect ourselves!"

"From what?" asked Wade. "That little bunny?"

"That was no little bunny!" Al-Ian yelled, still pushing the chest of drawers toward the front door. "That was a Cuddly Glowbunny from Planet Neon in the Glowstick Galaxy."

"So?" said Leyton.

"So, I told you," Al-Ian said. "The Cuddly Glowbunnies are the fiercest, most terrible killers in the whole universe!" Al-Ian stopped pushing the chest of drawers. His shoulders sagged and he hung his head. "Oh, what's the use? There's no point in trying to fight them. No planet has ever succeeded in stopping them. They're bound to win. We need a white sheet."

"Why?" asked TJ.

"To make a white flag and wave it outside so the Glowbunnies know we want to surrender," Al-Ian said. "We'll get down on our hands and knees and beg for mercy. We'll promise to be their slaves. We'll plead for our lives. We'll —"

"Uh, Al-Ian?" Wade interrupted.

"What?"

"It was just a little bunny," Wade said. "I mean, I know it glowed, but it really didn't look that scary."

"Exactly!" Al-Ian said. "That's how they do it! They look so cute and defenseless and the next thing you know, you're picking them up and cuddling them and petting them and then . . ." Al-Ian grabbed his head. "Oh. It's awful what they do. Just awful!"

"Have you actually *seen* what they do?" Wade asked.

"Of course not!" Al-Ian gasped. "No one has. At least no one who's *lived* to tell about it. The Cuddly Glowbunnies take no prisoners. They ravage and plunder and destroy everything in their path."

"Why?" asked TJ.

"Because," said Al-Ian.

"Because . . . ?" repeated Leyton.

"Because . . ." Al-Ian made a face. "I don't know. That's just what they do."

"If no one's seen them do it," said Wade, "or at least, lived to talk about it, how do you know it's true?"

"It just is," said Al-Ian.

Wade was no longer thinking about the terrible horrible things the Cuddly Glowbunnies might do to them. Instead he was thinking about all the candy they'd left on the sidewalk.

"I'm going back to get my candy," he said.

"*Are you crazy!!!?*" Al-Ian gasped.

Wade turned to TJ and Leyton. "You guys coming?"

"It's instant death," Al-Ian warned them. "If you guys set foot out there, you'll never come back."

"Well, I'm going," said Wade.

Leyton and TJ looked back and forth between Wade and Al-Ian. Like Wade, they really wanted their candy. But like Al-Ian, they were afraid of what the Cuddly Glowbunnies might do to them.

Wade reached for the doorknob.

"It's been nice knowing you, Wade," Al-Ian said. "Is there anything you'd like me to say at your funeral?"

Wade looked again at TJ and Leyton. "You guys want your candy or not?"

As scared as TJ and Leyton were, the thought of losing all those big red wax lips was even scarier. They headed for the door.

"Anything you want me to say at your funerals?" Al-Ian asked.

"Please say that I got smart," Leyton said. Then he and his brothers left.

It was dark outside and the shadowy streets were empty. It was past eight P.M., and trick-or-treating had officially ended. Even though Wade was pretty sure the glow-in-the-dark bunnies were not as dangerous as Al-Ian said, he was still nervous.

"You sure about this?" TJ whispered as they walked down the murky sidewalk.

"Pretty sure," said Wade, twisting his head this way and that in case any killer Cuddly Glowbunnies were hiding in the dark, waiting to attack.

"What if Al-Ian's right?" whispered Leyton.

"Then we're toast," said Wade. He thought he saw a flash of color to his right and stopped.

"*Oaf!*" Leyton, who was looking to his left, bumped into him.

"Watch where you're going!" Wade hissed.

"I'm scared," said TJ.

"Just chill, little dude," Wade said. They slowly made their way back to the spot where they'd seen the light blue glow-in-the-dark bunny.

Wade looked around. "Isn't this where we dropped the pillowcases?"

TJ looked around. "I think so."

"Me, too," said Leyton.

"So where's the candy?" Wade asked.

Leyton looked around and realized the terrible truth: The pillowcases full of candy were gone!

AN INVITATION TO INSTANT DEATH

"You think the Cuddly Glowbunnies took them?" Leyton asked.

Wade sighed unhappily. "Well, someone did."

"I bet that's what the Cuddly Glowbunnies do!" TJ exclaimed. "They travel around the universe taking over planets so they can steal Halloween candy!"

Wade had his doubts. "We might as well go back home," he said sadly. They walked back through the dark to their house and went up the front walk, past the broken bicycles, smashed skateboards, bent Razor scooters, partly burned sofas, and broken toilets. Leyton tried the front door. "It's locked."

Wade tried the door. "Al-Ian must have locked it." He knocked loudly. "Al-Ian!"

"Who is it?" Al-Ian asked from inside.

"Who do you think?" Wade said.

"Are you alone?" Al-Ian asked.

"No, I'm with Leyton and TJ," said Wade.

"Anyone else?" asked Al-Ian.

"No."

"You sure?"

Wade rolled his eyes. "Open the door, Al-Ian."

"What about the Cuddly Glowbunnies?" Al-Ian asked from the other side of the door. "Are they out there?"

"There are no Cuddly Glowbunnies out here," said Wade.

"How do I know they're not making you say that so that I'll open the door?" Al-Ian asked.

"I said there are no Cuddly Glowbunnies out here," Wade said firmly. "Now open the door. This is our house."

"Go away," said Al-Ian.

In the dark, outside the front door, the Tardy Boys shared frustrated looks.

"What do you think we should do, Leyton?" Wade asked.

Once again, Leyton was thrilled that his brother was asking for his help! The billions of brand-new, teensy-weensy, itsy-bitsy, baby brain cells began to jiggle and vibrate. *Boing!* A new idea popped into his head.

"Al-Ian?" Leyton said.

"What?" said Al-Ian from the other side of the door.

"Would you say the Cuddly Glowbunnies are proud aliens?" Leyton asked.

"Of course, they're proud," Al-Ian replied. "They're the fiercest, meanest, cruelest aliens in the universe. Why shouldn't they be proud?"

"Would you agree that they probably don't like it when people call them names?" Leyton asked.

"No way," said Al-Ian. "Calling the Cuddly Glowbunnies names would be an invitation to instant death."

"Then if the Cuddly Glowbunnies were outside with us," said Leyton, "and I started calling them names, I'd be in big trouble, right?"

"Definitely," said Al-Ian.

"Okay," said Leyton. Then in a loud voice he said, "Yo! Cuddly Glowbunnies. Your breath is so bad the dentist tried to wire your mouth shut. You're so ugly, when you look in the mirror your reflection barfs. You're so slow, you raced a pregnant lady and came in third. You're so dumb, you thought a quarterback was a refund."

Outside the front door, Leyton pressed a finger to his lips, warning his brothers to be quiet. A minute passed. And then another.

"Guys?" Al-Ian said in a low voice from the other side of the door.

Wade opened his mouth to answer, but Leyton quickly pressed his fingers to his lips.

"Hey, guys?" Al-Ian said a little more loudly.

The Tardy Boys didn't answer.

"Guys, you still there?" Al-Ian sounded nervous.

The Tardy Boys waited.

"Come on, guys," Al-Ian said anxiously. "If you're there, answer."

The Tardy Boys didn't answer.

"Please?" Al-Ian begged.

But the Tardy Boys said nothing.

Another minute passed.

Then the door clicked as Al-Ian unlocked it. He pulled it open just enough to peek out.

"Now!" Leyton yelled. He and his brothers rammed their shoulders against the door, knocking Al-Ian backward.

"You tricked me!" Al-Ian complained while the Tardy Boys entered the house.

"What did you expect?" Wade asked. "You wouldn't let us in our own house."

"I thought the Cuddly Glowbunnies were out there trying to get me," Al-Ian said.

"Forget about the Cuddly Glowbunnies," Wade grumbled.

"What are you talking about?" Al-Ian asked. "What about the light blue one we just saw?"

"Just because it was a bunny and it glowed doesn't make it a Cuddly Glowbunny," Wade said.

"Wait a minute," Al-Ian said. "Where's all the candy?"

"It wasn't there," said Leyton.

"The Cuddly Glowbunnies must have taken it!" Al-Ian gasped.

"That's what I said," said TJ.

Wade rolled his eyes. He'd had enough of the Cuddly Glowbunnies for now.

A
GOOD
EXCUSE

The next morning when Daisy knocked on the Tardy Boys' front door, Al-Ian answered it.

"What are you doing here?" she asked.

Al-Ian explained how he'd stayed at the Tardy Boys' house the previous night because he'd been too scared of the Cuddly Glowbunnies to go home. Then the Tardy Boys came to the door, and they all started to walk to The School With No Name.

Even though it was a beautiful, crisp fall day, the Tardy Boys hardly said a word. They walked with their heads bent and their shoulders slumped.

"What's wrong?" Daisy asked.

"We lost all our candy," Wade said, and told her how they'd finished trick-or-treating and were walking home when a light blue glow-in-the-dark bunny appeared and scared them away. And how, when they went back to look for their candy, it was gone.

"Are you saying you actually *saw* a real, live Cuddly Glowbunny?" asked Daisy.

"We definitely saw a glow-in-the-dark bunny," said Wade. "But I don't know if it was a Cuddly Glowbunny."

Suddenly they began to hear the

familiar shouts, screams, shrieks, yells, and screeches of Ulna Mandible. Ulna was shrieking at Principal Stratemeyer and Assistant Principal Snout. Meanwhile, Fibby hid behind her mother.

"I insist you have the janitor help my daughter carry her candy into school!" Ulna shouted. On a trailer behind Ulna's bright red Hummer was a candy-filled cardboard box about the size of a washing machine.

"I'm sorry, Mrs. Mandible," Principal Stratemeyer said calmly, "but our janitor is not required to help students bring their candy into school."

"If you don't help her, I'll sue!" Ulna threatened.

"On what grounds?" asked Assistant Principal Snout.

"On school grounds!" screamed Ulna.

When Fibby saw the Tardy Boys and their friends, she said, "Where's your candy?"

"We don't have any," Leyton answered sadly.

Fibby smiled happily. "Then you can't enter the King of Candy Contest! That means I'll have an even better chance of winning!"

Meanwhile, Ulna was still yelling at the principals. "If you won't help, then my daughter won't bring her candy to school!" She grabbed Fibby's hand and started to pull her toward the Hummer.

"What are you doing?" Fibby gasped.

"I'm taking you and all your candy home," Ulna said.

"Are you crazy?" Fibby pulled back. "I have to win the King of Candy Contest. If you can't make the janitor take my candy inside, then you'll have to do it yourself."

Ulna Mandible hung her head. She always did exactly what her daughter told her to do and if that meant carrying that giant box of candy into school, then she'd do it.

"And you better not drop it, either," Fibby warned.

Staggering under the weight of the huge box, Ulna carried it into school. Fibby followed. Principal Stratemeyer also went back into school. When Assistant Principal Snout saw the Tardy Boys and their friends, he checked his watch. "Late again! And don't try any of that 'maybe your watch is just early' stuff this time because I know my watch is right."

"How do you know?" asked Al-Ian.

"Because I checked it against Greenwich Mean Time," said the assistant principal. "The absolute measure of time as recorded by the atomic clock at the Royal Greenwich Observatory in Greenwich, England."

"But that's in England," said Al-Ian.

"Doesn't matter," said Assistant Principal Snout. "The atomic clock establishes the correct time for every time zone on Earth."

"Then how do you know you're in the right time zone?" asked Wade.

Assistant Principal Snout scowled. "It doesn't matter what time zone I'm in."

"But what if you're in one time zone and your watch is in another?" asked Leyton.

Assistant Principal Snout turned pale. "Is . . . that possible?"

Just then, Barton came down the

sidewalk pushing a large, square wheelbarrow filled with a mountain of candy.

"What about Barton?" asked Leyton. "If we're late, isn't he late, too?"

"Why are you late, Barton?" asked Assistant Principal Snout.

"I'm sorry, sir," Barton said. "I had no idea how hard it would be to bring all this candy to school. It took a lot longer than I expected."

"I'm not sure that's an acceptable excuse," said Assistant Principal Snout.

"But, sir, I could have brought a lot less candy and been on time, but then I wouldn't have as much to give to the candy charity," Barton said.

"So the reason you're late is because you want to give candy to charity?" said Assistant Principal Snout.

"Yes, sir," said Barton.

"That's very generous of you," said Assistant Principal Snout. "You can go into school."

Barton smiled meanly at the Tardy Boys and their friends.

"What about us?" asked Wade.

"I don't see you bringing any candy for charity," said Assistant Principal Snout.

"We would have, but someone stole it," said Wade.

"Yeah, right," Assistant Principal Snout scoffed. "You expect me to believe that? You four are getting a week's detention for being late, starting next week."

"But Barton was late, too," said Al-Ian.

"He had a good excuse," said Assistant Principal Snout.

The King of Candy Contest was held in the gym after school. Olga Shotput, the silver-medal-winning janitor, was in charge of weighing the candy. No one was surprised when Barton came in first and was officially crowned the King of Candy. Fibby came in second and her mother, Ulna, threw such a fit that Assistant

Principal Snout created a new category called Queen of Candy just for her.

As each contestant left the gym, they donated some candy to the big bright red plastic candy charity barrel (except Fibby, who kept every piece for herself). When everyone had left, Daisy asked the Tardy Boys and Al-Ian to help her wheel the barrel down to Ms. Fitt's room for safekeeping.

"Where is Ms. Fitt, anyway?" Al-Ian asked, noting that she had not attended the contest.

"She had to take Anestofleas to the veterinarian," said Daisy.

"Why would anyone take a nest of fleas to a veterinarian?" asked TJ, who'd come over from the elementary school to watch the contest.

"Not a nest of fleas," said Daisy. "Anestofleas. That's her cat's name."

"Ha-ha!" TJ laughed. "I get it. That's funny."

"Know what's *not* funny?" Wade asked.

"Saturday morning cartoons?" TJ guessed.

"No," said Wade.

"What's left of you after the Cuddly Glowbunnies are finished?" asked Al-Ian.

"No," said Wade. "What's not funny was Barton's candy."

"Because he had so much?" Daisy asked.

"No," said Wade. "Because I counted at least a dozen big red wax lips in that pile. I think he's the one who stole our candy. And I bet he used that glow-in-the-dark bunny to do it."

"Are you saying that Barton is working

with the Cuddly Glowbunnies?" Al-Ian gasped.

"No —" Wade started to say. "That's not what I —"

"It makes perfect sense!" Al-Ian cried. "The Cuddly Glowbunnies always use spies! Barton's their spy!"

"Why would Barton spy for the Cuddly Glowbunnies?" Daisy asked.

"They must have made a deal with him," Al-Ian said. "He spied for them and they made sure he won the King of Candy Contest and got all that candy. And that means Barton doesn't have a glowologist aunt! The Cuddly Glowbunnies made that lightbulb costume for him. That was part of the deal!"

Wade bit his lip nervously. For the first time, Al-Ian's theories were starting to make sense.

"Seriously, Wade," Al-Ian said. "Have you ever heard of a glowologist? There's no such thing. It's been the Cuddly Glowbunnies all along!"

Wade glanced at Daisy to see what she thought. "I have to admit," she said. "It does make sense."

"You see!" Al-Ian cried. "That'll teach you to make fun of me!"

Wade was really starting to worry. If Al-Ian was right and the Cuddly Glowbunnies had hired Barton as their spy, that meant they planned to take over the Earth and do terrible things to everyone. Wade wondered what Leyton thought. Now that his brother's head was filled with billions of brand-new, teensy-weensy, itsy-bitsy, baby brain cells he was a good person to ask. But Leyton had stopped down the hall to read some of the poetry essays Ms. Fitt had stuck on the wall outside her room.

"Leyton," Wade called. "Do you think Al-Ian's right about Barton being a spy for the Cuddly Glowbunnies?"

"I don't know," said Leyton. "But here's something strange. Someone else spells *pretty* wrong."

The others came over to look. Leyton had turned to the last page of an essay, where the author had written the following:

In conclusion, I'd just like to say that I picked this guy Dante to write about because the school nurse Ms. Take said he was the greatest poet who ever lived. But frankly, I think The Divine Comedy is a joke. I mean, who writes a poem that is three books long? That alone is pritty ridiculous. . . .

"Oh, my gosh!" Daisy gasped. "Do you know what this means?"

"It's a bad idea to ask the school nurse about poetry?" Al-Ian guessed.

"No, the person who wrote this essay must be my secret admirer." Daisy flipped through the pages until she came to the front of the essay. "It's Barton!" she gasped.

"Of course!" Al-Ian realized. "It makes perfect sense!" He spun around and dashed down the hall and out of school.

"Where's he going?" Leyton asked.

"I don't know," said Wade. Then he narrowed his eyes. "But I just figured out how we can get all our candy back. Come on, we have to run!"

ARE YOU NOW OR HAVE YOU EVER BEEN?

While Daisy stayed behind to lock the charity candy barrel in Ms. Fitt's room, the Tardy Boys raced out of school.

"Why are we running?" TJ asked as they sprinted outside.

"Don't you want your candy back?" Wade asked, and pointed down the block. "There he is!" Ahead on the sidewalk, they could see Barton pushing his wheelbarrow filled with candy.

"Hey!" Wade said.

Barton stopped. When he saw the Tardy Boys coming toward him, he set his jaw firmly and narrowed his eyes.

"Stay away from my candy!" he warned.

"It's not yours," Wade said. "Most of it's ours. You stole it from us."

"Did not," Barton said.

"Oh, yeah?" said Leyton. "Then where'd you get all those wax lips?"

"How should I know?" Barton said. "You think I keep track of where every piece of candy came from?"

"Spell *pretty*," said Wade.

"P-R-I-T-T-Y," said Barton.

The Tardy Boys grinned. "We know you're the secret admirer who's been writing love poems to Daisy," Wade said.

Barton went pale. "How?"

"You always spell *pretty* P-R-I-T-T-Y when it's really spelled P-R-E-T-T-Y," said Leyton.

"Darn, I should have used a dictionary," Barton muttered.

"If you don't give us back our candy, we'll tell the whole school," said Wade.

"Okay, okay, I'll give you the wax lips," said Barton.

"Not just the wax lips," said Wade. "All our candy. Three pillowcases full."

Barton turned even paler. "But then I'll hardly have any left."

"You'll just have to wait until next year," said Wade. "When you can spend more time trick-or-treating and less time scheming how to steal candy from other people."

"How do I know you won't take your

candy back and still show everyone those poems?" Barton asked. "I'm not giving you your candy until I get those poems back."

Wade thought about it. "Here's the deal. Tomorrow morning before school, we'll meet right here. I'll bring the poems. And you bring our candy. But in the meantime, no tricks?"

"No tricks," said Barton.

"Pinkie swear?" Wade held out his pinkie.

"Oh, okay." Barton sighed and linked pinkies. Then he picked up his wheelbarrow and started toward home.

"Just one last thing," Leyton said.

Barton glared at him. "Now what?!"

"Are you now, or have you ever been, a spy for the Cuddly Glowbunnies?"

Barton rolled his eyes and turned away.

SERIOUS STUFF

That night, the Tardy Boys went over to Daisy's house and got the poems. The next morning, they met Barton and made the exchange. They took their pillowcases of candy home and then hurried to school.

Later that day, Ms. Fitt asked if anyone wanted to do their oral poem analysis. Al-Ian raised his hand and went to the front of the class.

"To analyze a poem means to figure out what it *really* means instead of what it sounds like it means," he told the class. "I know some kids may think this is kind of pointless, but I think it's really important."

At her desk, Ms. Fitt smiled.

"Let me give you an example of how important this can be," Al-Ian continued. "Recently our planet was visited by the Cuddly Glowbunnies from Planet Neon in the Glowstick Galaxy. Normally, this would be cause for great alarm because the Glowbunnies are the cruelest, meanest, most ruthless killers in the entire universe."

Around the classroom kids began to smile.

"The good news is that the Cuddly Glowbunnies have been sending us messages of peace," said Al-Ian. "These messages have been disguised inside love poems to Daisy Peduncle from Barton Slugg."

A ripple of whispers raced through the class, and then kids started to giggle and stare at Barton.

"No, no!" said Al-Ian. "Don't laugh. This is *really* serious. You have no idea how lucky we are. If the Cuddly Glowbunnies wanted to, they could have made us all their slaves . . . or worse!"

But the class kept chuckling and Barton's face grew bright red. Even Ms. Fitt grinned. "Al-Ian," she said. "Are you sure this is serious?"

"I'm positive," Al-Ian insisted, holding up some sheets of paper. "I have copies of the poems right here. The first one is titled 'To Daisy from a Secret Admirer.' Obviously the Cuddly Glowbunnies are pretending to be the secret admirer because they don't want us to know who they really are. And now listen to this." He read:

Every day at school when you walk by
I feel an ache in my heart and the need to sigh.
It kills me that I cannot not talk to you.
I wish every day I could walk with you.

Al-Ian stopped reading and spoke to the class. "This means that the Cuddly Glowbunnies knew that if they tried to contact us directly we would freak out and assume they were going to attack. And when they say they wish they could walk with us, that's a peace offering."

Al-Ian looked toward Ms. Fitt, who nodded. "I must say that's a very interesting interpretation, Al-Ian."

Al-Ian turned to the class. "Okay, now here's the next part of the poem:

> You are the sweetest girl in the whole school.
> Anyone who doesn't know that is a fool.
> Even if we lived in the biggest, most crowded city
> There would never be another girl as pritty.

Once again, the class started giggling.

"Guys, this isn't funny," Al-Ian told them. "I think the Cuddly Glowbunnies are using metaphors here. When they say, 'You are the sweetest girl in the whole school,' they're not talking about Daisy. They're talking about *all* humans. And school is a metaphor for the universe. So what they're really saying is that humans are the best species in the whole universe. I mean, except for the Cuddly

Glowbunnies themselves. And they want to be our friends."

Giggles and chuckles kept popping up here and there, but Ms. Fitt frowned at the students and nodded at Al-Ian to continue. He read the second poem, singling out phrases like

You and I would make a wonderful pair.
Together there is nothing we couldn't do
We could conquer the world if we wanted to.
Tear down great buildings; turn day to night.

and

And the world will be ours once and for all.
And I will be your boyfriend, even though I'm
not tall.

"This means the Cuddly Glowbunnies want us to join them in conquering the universe," Al-Ian explained. "They're saying they need us because they're short and furry and we're tall and, well, not furry."

Barton's face was still bright red.

The class laughed and giggled until Ms. Fitt stood up and sternly said, "That's enough. That was excellent, Al-Ian. I think you did a wonderful job of analyzing those poems."

The bell rang. Kids started to get up and leave. Barton stayed at his desk and pretended to read a book. But he was holding it so tight that his knuckles had turned white.

Out in the hall, the Tardy Boys and Al-Ian stopped by Wade's locker. Leyton and Wade were grinning.

"Why did everyone think it was so funny?" Al-Ian asked. "Don't they understand how lucky we are that the Cuddly Glowbunnies want to be our friends?"

"Dude, what if they're not Cuddly Glowbunnies?" Wade asked.

Al-Ian frowned. "Are you going to start this again? Yesterday afternoon in the hall outside Ms. Fitt's room you were convinced. Face it. The only glowing bunnies in the universe are the Cuddly Glowbunnies. And we just happen to be incredibly lucky that they want to be our friends."

Just then a voice said, "Too bad, Al-Ian, your luck just ran out."

WHAT BUNNIES LOVE

Barton was standing behind Al-Ian. His face was still bright red, his hands were clenched into fists, and he was grinding his teeth with anger. "You're going to be so sorry."

"But you don't understand," said Al-Ian. "Everyone should be thanking you. You helped the Earth get the message that the

Cuddly Glowbunnies don't want to destroy us."

The nastiest, meanest grin ever appeared on Barton's lips. "That's what you think. I'm going to tell my Glowbunny friends to make sure you never embarrass me again. If I were you, I'd go back to your house right now and never, ever leave." He stormed away.

Al-Ian turned pale and started to tremble. Just then Daisy came around the corner. Seeing Al-Ian she said, "Why are you pale and trembling?"

"Barton's going to tell the Cuddly Glowbunnies to get me," Al-Ian stammered.

"But what if there are no Cuddly Glowbunnies?" Daisy asked.

"Of course there are!" Al-Ian cried. "Come on, guys, we've been over this a hundred times. Barton just admitted that he's been working with them. This is terrible. I have to go home!"

"Al-Ian, wait!" Wade called. But it was too late. Fearing for his life, Al-Ian ran away down the hall.

"He really believes the Cuddly Glowbunnies are going to get him," said Wade.

"Why would Barton threaten to tell the Cuddly Glowbunnies if they don't exist?" Daisy asked.

It was a good question, and Wade turned to Leyton to see if he had an answer. Leyton's skull started to vibrate, as if the brand-new, baby brain cells were jumping around like a billion teensy-weensy, itsy-bitsy jumping beans. He could feel an idea coming. And it wasn't just any idea. It was a REALLY BIG IDEA!

Ka-boing!

"Barton knows how scared Al-Ian is of the Cuddly Glowbunnies," he said. "I'll bet he told Al-Ian to go home because he plans to let a bunch of them go around Al-Ian's house!"

"That would scare Al-Ian to death," said Wade.

"Wait a minute," Daisy said. "I'm confused. Are they Cuddly Glowbunnies or just glow-in-the-dark bunnies?"

"Doesn't matter," said Wade. "Either one's going to freak Al-Ian out completely."

"But if they're not Cuddly Glowbunnies, then how can they glow in the dark?" Daisy asked.

"We don't know," said Wade. "But we have to stop Barton."

"How?" asked Daisy.

Wade thought about it. "What's the one thing bunnies love more than anything else?"

"Other bunnies?" Leyton guessed.

"No. Carrots," said Wade. He turned to Daisy. "Do you have any of those organic carrots left over from Halloween?"

"Almost all of them," said Daisy.

THE
RAB-O-TRAP

As soon as school ended, the Tardy Boys hurried to Daisy's to pick up the carrots. Daisy had spent the afternoon in the school library and now her forehead was wrinkled and she looked very upset. "I think I know where those glow-in-the-dark bunnies came from," she said in her kitchen. "Do you know about Gene Splicing?"

"Never heard of her," said Leyton.

"It's not a person," said Daisy. "It's something scientists do in laboratories. They experiment on defenseless little bunnies, mixing their cells with the cells of jellyfish and other things that glow in the dark. It's terrible."

"Sounds bad," said Wade. "So, can we get some of those organic carrots?"

"First I need to know what you intend to do with the glow-in-the-dark bunnies if you catch them," Daisy said.

Wade and Leyton scratched their heads. They'd been so busy thinking about how to get the bunnies before Al-Ian saw them, that they hadn't thought about what they would do with the bunnies.

"What do you think we should do?" asked Wade.

"I'm going to call CARROT," Daisy said.

"Carrots have telephones?" asked TJ, who had just walked over, looking for his brothers.

"C-A-R-R-O-T is the name of an organization," Daisy explained. "It stands for Caring Americans who Rescue Rabbits On Tuesdays."

"Why can't they rescue rabbits on Mondays?" asked TJ.

"Because then they'd be called CARROM," said Daisy.

"But then can't they rescue rabbits on Thursdays as well?" asked Wade.

"On Thursdays, they rescue raccoons," said Daisy.

"So they're also called CARROT on Thursdays?" Leyton asked.

"Precisely," said Daisy. She opened the refrigerator and took out a big bag of organic carrots. But before she gave them to the Tardy Boys, she said, "You have to promise me that nothing bad will happen to those bunnies. Can you keep them safe until Tuesday when the people from CARROT come to rescue them?"

"We promise," said Wade.

A few minutes later, the Tardy Boys left Daisy's with the bag of organic carrots.

"When do you want to go to Al-Ian's house?" Leyton asked.

"Just before dark," said Wade.

"How are we going to catch the rabbits?" TJ asked. "Won't we need some kind of trap?"

"Or a really big vacuum cleaner," said Leyton. "The Rab-o-Vac."

"We don't have a Rab-o-Vac," said Wade.

"How about a really big rake?" asked Leyton. "The Rab-o-Rake."

"I once saw this cartoon where they propped a box open with a stick and put bait under the box," TJ said. "The stick was attached to a string and when the animal went under the box to eat the bait, someone would pull the string and the box closed with the animal inside."

"The Rab-o-Trap!" said Leyton.

"That's it," said Wade.

Back at their house, the Tardy Boys made Rab-o-Traps out of boxes, sticks, and string. Then, just before dark, they went to Al-Ian's house and placed half a dozen traps around the yard, baiting them with Daisy's organic carrots.

"What if the glow-in-the-dark bunnies don't come?" Leyton whispered while he and his brothers hid behind a bush with the strings in their hands.

"Then we'll go home," Wade whispered back.

"What if the Cuddly Glowbunnies come instead?" asked TJ.

"Then we'll *run* home," said Wade.

Sure enough, as soon as it got dark, glow-in-the dark bunnies began to appear on Al-Ian's lawn. Some were pink, some green, and some blue. Each time one got near a Rab-o-Trap, its little glow-in-the-dark nose would begin to twitch and it would go straight for Daisy's organic carrot.

Thump! One of the boys pulled a string and the box fell, capturing a bunny. After a while, no new glow-in-the-dark bunnies appeared, and the Tardy Boys collected the bunnies and headed home.

"Now all we have to do is keep them

somewhere until Tuesday when the people from CARROT come," Wade said when they got back to their house.

The Tardy Boys decided to keep the glow-in-the-dark bunnies in the kitchen. When Wade went to bed that night, he figured that over the weekend they would feed the rabbits organic carrots and play with them. Then on Tuesday, the CARROT people would come and take them, and everyone would live happily ever after.

Knock! Knock! Knock! The next morning, Wade was awakened by a loud knocking at the front door. He could hear voices coming from outside. When he pulled back the window shade, he couldn't believe what he saw. Parked on the street were TV vans and cars from radio stations and newspapers. Dozens of media people were standing on the sidewalk and front lawn. Some were taking photos of the broken bicycles, smashed skateboards, bent Razor scooters, partly burned sofas, and broken toilets scattered around the yard. Others were stopping the Tardy Boys' neighbors and interviewing them.

Knock! Knock! Knock! The banging continued on the front door. Wade pulled on some clothes and went out into the hall. Leyton and TJ were just coming out of their rooms.

"What's going on?" TJ asked.

"It's the media," said Wade.

"What do they want?" asked Leyton.

Knock! Knock! Knock!

"We better go see," said Wade.

They went downstairs, and Wade opened the front door a little. A bunch of reporters with microphones and video cameras pressed forward, blinding the boys with camera lights and shoving digital recorders in their faces.

"Where are the bunnies?" demanded a woman with blonde hair.

"Do they really glow in the dark?" asked a man wearing a tie and jacket.

"Is it true they come from outer space?" asked a guy with a video camera on his shoulder.

BUNNY MATH

Wade slammed the door closed.

"How did they find out about the bunnies?" TJ asked.

"Barton must have told them," said Wade.

"What should we do?" asked TJ.

"Maybe if we ignore them they'll go away," said Leyton.

"Good idea," said Wade.

The boys went into the kitchen where the glow-in-the-dark bunnies were hopping around, twitching their little glow-in-the-dark noses.

"Hey, that's weird," said Leyton. "Last night, there were six bunnies. Now there are eight."

"They must be multiplying!" Wade realized.

"Bunnies know math?" TJ asked with a puzzled look.

"Uh, not exactly," said Wade.

Knock! Knock! Knock! The media people outside kept knocking. TJ and Leyton tried to watch cartoons, and Wade tried to study vocabulary, but the noise was too distracting.

Then the telephone rang. Wade answered, "Hello?"

"What colors do they glow?" a voice asked.

Wade hung up the phone, but it immediately started to ring again. Wade couldn't study. He went into the den where TJ and Leyton were watching cartoons. He could see that his brothers were having a hard time concentrating on the TV. Every time someone knocked on the door, or the phone rang, Leyton and TJ would glance toward the windows.

"Guys, this is driving me crazy," Wade said.

"Us, too," said Leyton.

"We have to do something," said Wade.

"Like what?" asked TJ.

"I don't know," Wade said. "I have a feeling those media people are going to stay out there until we show them the rabbits. But if we do that, they're going to want to take them away. And we promised Daisy we wouldn't let anything bad happen to them."

"So what can we do?" TJ asked.

Wade looked at Leyton. "Can you think of anything?"

Leyton concentrated. All the brand-new, teensy-weensy, itsy-bitsy, baby brain cells in his skull had recently awakened from a long night's sleep, and they were feeling refreshed and energetic. So they were happy to start jiggling and vibrating.

Boing!

Once again, Leyton had an idea!

THE
HIDDEN
BUNNY
TRICK

A little while later, Wade opened the front door. Outside, all the reporters and TV and radio people crowded toward him.

"Are you ready to speak to us?" asked a woman with dark hair.

"Are you ready to show us the glow-in-the-dark bunnies?" asked a cameraman with a brown beard.

"I'm sorry," said Wade, "but there are no glow-in-the-dark bunnies here."

The crowd stared at him in stunned silence. Then a man wearing a green vest said, "We don't believe you!"

"If that's true, why won't you let us in?" asked a woman wearing a gray suit.

"You're welcome to come in," Wade said, and held the door open.

The crowd of media people rushed into the house with their cameras and microphones. They searched everywhere, starting on the first floor and going up to the second floor. When they couldn't find any glow-in-the-dark bunnies, they searched the attic. But the glow-in-the-dark bunnies weren't there.

"What about the basement?" asked the woman in the gray suit.

"Forget it," said a man wearing a tie and

jacket. "These houses don't have basements."

The reporters and media people hung their heads in disappointment. Their shoulders drooped sadly.

"It was just a big hoax," said the woman with blonde hair.

"What a waste of time," muttered the man in the green vest.

"If I ever find the kid who called in this story, I'll wring his neck," muttered the woman with dark hair.

The media people left. Wade stood by the door and said good-bye. Just as the last reporter was leaving, Daisy came up the walk wearing a bright green-and-red wool poncho.

"What were all those media people doing here?" she whispered to Wade.

"Looking for the glow-in-the-dark bunnies," Wade whispered back.

"Oh, no!" Daisy looked horrified. "Did they find them?"

Wade shook his head. "Nope, thanks to Leyton's brilliant idea, the bunnies are safe." He let Daisy into the house, then closed the door and said, "Okay, Leyton, you can let them out."

In the kitchen, Leyton opened the trapdoor to the basement, and all the glow-in-the-dark bunnies scampered out.

"Hiding the bunnies we don't have, in the basement we don't have, was a great idea!" Wade said with a laugh as he slapped Leyton's palm.

"And you thought of it," Daisy said to Leyton.

Leyton smiled proudly. This was the best proof yet that the brand-new brain cells in his skull were growing bigger and stronger and having all sorts of terrific ideas!

"This is so wonderful!" Daisy gushed as the glow-in-the-dark bunnies scampered around her feet. "Now the people from CARROT can give these unique and delightful little creatures a nice safe home where they can live happily forever after."

"And multiply and divide and maybe even learn fractions!" TJ added.

Knock! Knock! Knock! But just then there was another knock at the door!

THE
OMINOUS
DR. SLUGG

The Tardy Boys and Daisy stared at one another in fear.

"What if it's more media people?" Daisy whispered.

"What if they've figured out that we *do* have a basement?" Leyton said. "There isn't time to gather up all the bunnies and find a new place to hide them."

Knock! Knock! Knock!

"TJ, go see who it is," Wade whispered while he, Leyton, and Daisy waited in the kitchen.

TJ went to the door and then returned to the kitchen. "It's a woman with white hair," he said in a low voice. "She wants the glow-in-the-dark bunnies. I told her that all the reporters and TV people had just searched the house and didn't find a single bunny. But she said she knows they're here."

Wade's jaw dropped. He looked at Leyton and Daisy. "What should we do?"

Knock! Knock! Knock!

"That's her again," said TJ. "She said she won't leave until she gets her bunnies back."

"Wait a minute," said Daisy. "Did she really say they were *her* bunnies?"

"That's what she said," said TJ.

Daisy turned to Wade and Leyton and said, "If they're her bunnies, then we have to give them back."

"But what if they're not really hers?" asked Leyton.

"Was she alone?" Wade asked TJ.

TJ nodded. "All the media people left."

"Maybe we should go talk to her," Wade said.

They went to the front door. Outside was a short woman with white hair falling down on her forehead and buck teeth. She looked oddly familiar.

"Hello," she said. "I've come for my rabbits."

"Who are you?" Daisy asked.

"Doctor Ima Slugg, the world's foremost expert in glowology."

"You're Barton's aunt!" Leyton realized.

"Yes, I'm afraid that's true," said Dr. Slugg.

"Why have you been experimenting on bunnies?" Daisy asked. "Isn't that mean and cruel?"

"I don't think so," said Dr. Slugg. "I keep them outside where they can run around. The bunnies seem to be happy. I don't think they care that they glow."

"Why invent glow-in-the-dark bunnies in the first place?" asked Wade.

"I did it for my nephew Barton," said Dr. Slugg. "You see, he's afraid of the dark. But he feels too old for a night-light. I thought if I invented a glow-in-the-dark bunny, he could keep one in his room as a pet, and no one would realize that it was also a night-light."

"Isn't Barton a little old to be afraid of the dark?" TJ asked.

"He's a little old to be watching *Power Rangers*, too," Dr. Slugg said with a shrug. "But what can I do? He's my nephew."

"And how come we kept seeing glow-in-the-dark bunnies around our neighborhood?" asked Leyton.

"My fence is old and they keep escaping," Dr. Slugg said. "Except last night when Barton took them on purpose. Now, can I please have my bunnies back?"

THE END

The mystery of the glow-in-the-dark bunnies was solved. That afternoon, the Tardy Boys, Daisy, and Al-Ian celebrated by sitting around the Tardy Boys' kitchen table, eating Halloween candy (except for Daisy, who ate an apple).

"So they weren't Cuddly Glowbunnies after all," said TJ as he chewed on a Tootsie Roll.

"I'm still not sure," said Al-Ian, who was sucking on a giant jawbreaker. "They could have been Cuddly Glowbunnies who were just pretending to be regular old glow-in-the-dark bunnies."

"Well, I just want to say that what impressed me the most about our recent adventure is how many great ideas my brother Leyton came up with," Wade said, savoring a raspberry Shock Tart.

Even though his mouth was stuffed with red wax lips, Leyton beamed proudly. "I cooffn't haff done it wiffout Daify."

"Why?" asked TJ.

Leyton chewed the wax lips until he could speak clearly. "Because she told me all about Brain Food. And once I started eating it, billions of brand-new, teensy-weensy, itsy-bitsy, baby brain cells started growing in my skull and giving me ideas."

Wade frowned. "But Brain Food is fish. And you never eat fish."

"Sure I do." Leyton went over to the kitchen cabinets and took out packages of Goldfish crackers and Swedish Gummi Fish and fish-shaped chocolates. "See, all this stuff is fish."

Wade groaned and shook his head. "Dude, that's not fish. That's just food *shaped* like fish."

"Do you mean I was supposed to eat *real* fish?" Leyton gasped in horror. "But I *hate* fish!"

Daisy grinned and nodded. But Leyton felt terrible.

"Why are you smiling?" he asked her. "This is awful! If I wasn't eating real Brain Food all this time, then I haven't been growing real brain cells! That means my skull is still empty."

"That's not what it means at all," said Daisy. "It means that you've always had brains."

"No, I haven't," said Leyton. "All I had were vast empty spaces where monkeys could swing from the branches of trees."

"You're wrong, Leyton," insisted Daisy. "You have brains. You just didn't know it. That's why you had all those wonderful ideas even though you didn't eat real Brain Food."

Leyton's jaw fell open and he stared at Wade. "Is it true?"

"It must be," said Wade. "Brain Food or not, you came up with those ideas."

"Does that mean I can be TOTALLY BEYOND EXCELLENT IN SCHOOL and get a scholarship to college?" Leyton asked excitedly.

"If you study really hard," said Daisy.

"Awesome!" Leyton stood up and got his shovel out of the closet. "I'm going to start studying hard," he said. "Just as soon as I finish digging the basement and put in some windows."

(SOME STUFF AFTER) THE END

This book is a work of fiction. That means the author made most of it up. But some of it is also true. For example, glow-in-the-dark bunnies actually exist. So do glow-in-the-dark fish and pigs.

It is also true that kids used to eat candies like big red wax lips and little wax bottles filled with flavored syrups. Back in those days, a kid could go to the drugstore and sit on a stool at the counter and have a milk shake made from real milk and ice cream. You can still do that at the Yellowstone Drug Store in Shoshone, Wyoming.

The author knows this is true because that's where Catherine Zeta-Jones said she'd meet him but never showed up. Shame on you, Catherine Zeta-Jones. The author waited for three days and gained eighteen pounds drinking milk shakes. While he was waiting, he decided to start the next book in this series, *Is That an Angry Penguin in Your Hockey Bag?* He would like to dedicate it to Scarlett Johansson. Does anyone know her phone number?

If you liked this book, you'll LOVE these STINKY ADVENTURES!

IS That a Dead Dog in Your Locker?

When Leyton and Wade Tardy agree to help their friend Daisy hide a dog at school, they have no idea what they're getting themselves into! Wheezy is just a small dog, but he leaves a BIG stink behind wherever he goes. Can Wade and Leyton keep Wheezy a secret, or will his awful stench give him away?

IS That a Sick Cat in Your Backpack?

Leyton and Wade Tardy's pet cat Skinny Cat has one very big, very disgusting talent—he can cough up hair balls like a champ! But will that be enough for him to win the school's Catalent Contest?